TREASURE OF THE BRASADA

Being caught, bloody gun in hand, leaning over the body of the man he had threatened to kill forces broncobuster Glenn Crawford to turn up at the Big O ranch, a weary, footsore fugitive with more than one score to settle.

Even the murder of the ranch owner in San Antonio had not prepared Crawford for the state of affairs he finds at the ranch. His sudden presence there seems to scare some of the crew half to death and lead others to try to kill him every chance they get.

For the moment, however, Crawford is more interested in the state of affairs in his own body than those of the Big O and the murderer he is sure the ranch harbors.

TREASURE OF THE BRASADA

Les Savage, Jr.

W
FIC
SAU
c.1

This hardback edition 1999
by Chivers Press
by arrangement with
Golden West Literary Agency

ISBN 0 7540 8073 0

British Library Cataloguing in Publication Data available

Printed and bound in Great Britain by
Redwood Books, Trowbridge, Wiltshire

TREASURE OF THE BRASADA

List of Chapters—

Treasure of the Brasada

Chapter One

CIRCUMSTANTIAL EVIDENCE

CROSSING ALAMO PLAZA, Glenn Crawford was almost to the Manger Hotel when he became aware of Sheriff Ed Kenmare standing in the entrance to the patio. Crawford felt the hesitant break to his stride. Then, deliberately, he went on, feeling for the first time the sweat glistening on his unshaven upper lip and forming dark blue spots in the armpits of his faded ducking jacket. It might have been the sun. It was a hot spring for San Antonio.

"How about the riding, Glenn?" asked the sheriff, casually.

"My legs are all right, Ed," said Crawford, halting momentarily.

"I noticed you still limped a bit," Kenmare told him. "You got off easy, I guess. Horse mashed my cousin's legs rolling on him that way up in Deaf Smith. He never did heal so he could ride any more."

"My legs are all right," said Crawford, turning to go past him and through the patio gate.

"You got other things to heal besides your legs," said Kenmare, shifting his dusty, tobacco-odored bulk in front of Crawford. "Why don't you think things out a bit longer before you see Otis Rockland again?"

"This isn't my idea," said Crawford. "Otis sent me word he was here and wanted to talk."

Kenmare's watery gray eyes met Crawford's, and he put a gnarled hand on the younger man's arm. "Then give me your gun, Glenn, before you go up."

A strange, defiant withdrawal drew Crawford's body

up, accentuating for the first time its restless, animal
lines. In his brass-studded levis, he had the lean catty legs
and negligible hips of a man whose work had been much
in the saddle, and though his shoulders were narrow,
their muscularity was apparent beneath the denim jacket.
His forehead was high and bony and pale below the short
curling black hair; and, set deep within their sockets, his
eyes held a sunken, almost feverish glow, which could
have come from the recent sickness, or something else.
His rope-marked fingers tightened about the brass re-
ceiver of his old Henry.

"I'll keep the rifle, Ed," he said. "Now let me by."

Kenmare did not release Crawford's arm. He dropped
his gaze to one side, reaching up to rub the sweat exuding
from the large, greasy pores of his rather bulbous nose.

"Something I never did get straight, Glenn," he said,
looking at the worn boot he was scuffing in the earth.
"This whole thing between you and Rockland seems to
have started with the way Rockland got hold of Delcazar's land."

"Del was—"

"I know, Glenn, I know." Kenmare's fingers tightened
momentarily on Crawford's arm. "You and Delcazar
was pretty close friends. And you think Rockland gave
Delcazar a raw deal."

"You know he did," said Crawford. "Del had a small
spread, but it had the best water in that section of the
brush. Rockland had to have that water. And he got it."

"But he did it all legal, Glenn."

"Legal." Crawford's voice was bitter. "He knew Del
only held his spread with one of those old Spanish grants
they call a *sitio*. His lawyers found out that this one was
so mixed up through the years that Del couldn't prove
ownership. He petitioned the state, had it declared pub-
lic domain, and got it for a song. Yes, it was legal all
right."

"Those things happen," said Kenmare wearily. "It wasn't your spread, Glenn."

"No. But Del was my friend. I was busting broncs for Otis Rockland at the time. I went to him and told—"

That hand tightened again. "I know what you told him, Glenn. Maybe you were right. Maybe Rockland even had that cinch cut on the black killer so it would roll you. But listen, Glenn—" Kenmare took a weary, wheezing breath—"this ain't the way."

"What isn't the way?" said Crawford with growing heat. "I told you Rockland sent for me, Ed."

"There must have been half a dozen Big O hands heard you threaten to kill Rockland after that bronc rolled you under," Kenmare told him heavily.

"Don't you think three months in the hospital cools a man off some, Ed?" said Crawford. "Now get out of my way. It's too hot for an argument. I'll buy you a beer on the way out."

He shoved past the sheriff and into the tiled patio. The alamo tree dropped its deep, dappled shade over the cattlemen sitting tilted back in the line of peeling cane chairs against the adobe wall. Their lazy, sporadic conversation died abruptly, and the only sound was the hard beat of Crawford's heels against the tiles. His lips formed a thin, bitter line against his teeth as he passed the speculation in their lifted gazes and entered the foyer. The cool, inner chill struck him with a distinct physical force, after the stifling heat of the day without, and caused him to draw in a quick breath. He skirted a potted palm and went up the broad, carpeted stairs to 211, the room Otis Rockland always took when he came to San Antonio.

He had lifted his hand to knock, when the sound came from inside. It was muffled and dim at first, rising to a thumping crescendo, with someone calling something, the whole thing ceasing then, abruptly. After a moment of silence, Crawford seemed to hear heavy breathing. He let his knuckles strike the pine panel of the door. It rattled mutedly. That was his only answer.

"Otis?" he called.

He waited a moment longer, then turned the knob. The door opened into the sumptuous parlor of the suite. The wine overhangings were drawn across the windows against the sun, casting into semi-gloom the spidery pattern of white and gilt furniture in the room. He heard a shutter clack in the bedroom and knocked his knee against a low marquetry table in front of the sofa as he headed for the door. He took his Henry in both hands and shoved open the door with its tip. The first thing he saw was a pile of blue chintz on the floor. It was the hanging, torn off the tester of the four-poster, and Otis Rockland must have clutched it when falling, for his hand was still gripping it in terrifying desperation. The portieres had been pulled back by an opened shutter, and the avenue of bright light, splashing across the rich Brussels carpet, touched Rockland's feet and led Crawford to turn momentarily toward the window.

"No—Crawford—"

He wheeled back to see Rockland's eyes open. The man made some feeble effort to rise. Crawford dropped to one knee beside him, laying the rifle down.

"Delcazar?" he said.

Rockland's lips twisted in what could have been a smile.

"Like you, to think of that."

"I guess more than one has good cause to want you dead, Otis," said Crawford.

"Yes." It came out of the man in a hoarse, strained way. But there was a look of macabre humor or malice, or both, in his face as he spoke. "They'll think it was Delcazar, won't they? Or you, Glenn."

"I'll get someone—"

"No. No." Rockland reached up to grab at his shirt as Crawford started to rise. "Won't do any good. Too late." He fought for breath for a moment, then went on, slowly. "Reach—inside—coat."

Crawford could see the thick, viscid blood forming beneath the back of Rockland's iron-gray head now. There was a brutal slash across the man's face, slicing deep into the bridge of his dominating, avaricious nose. Even as Crawford watched, the eyes closed and the breathing grew stertorous. The man was obviously beyond help. With a swift movement Crawford reached beneath Rockland's expensive steel pen, drawing a wallet from the inner pocket. He was starting to go through it, when Rockland's eyes opened.

"Rip lining, Glenn," he whispered. "What he was after—you scared him off—'fore he could find it."

Crawford fumbled with the soft doeskin flap of the wallet, finally managing to rip it out, revealing a piece of faded, yellowed paper. He pulled this out. Unfolded, it formed a triangle, the bottom straight, the other two sides jagged and torn. "Looks like some kind of a map," he said.

"Yes," said Rockland, feebly. "*Derrotero*. Santa Anna's chests."

"Whose chests? What are you talking about, Otis?"

Rockland's lip drew back over his teeth, more a grimace than a smile. "Don't lie, Crawford," he murmured. "Why else were you so het-up when I got Delcazar's spread? You knew about this *derrotero* then."

"About what?" said Crawford hotly, clutching him. "How is Del mixed up in this?"

But Rockland's head had fallen back once more; and for a moment Crawford thought he was gone. Suddenly he found himself shaking Rockland in a fever of impatience. "Otis," he cried, "Otis, did Del give you this? Where did you get this map?"

Once more Rockland's eyes opened, but a glaze was on them. "Mexico," he whispered. "Mexico City."

Suddenly Crawford knew. The Delcazars had come from Mexico City originally. And their family papers must have been in the hands of a lawyer there. When Rockland got Delcazar's spread, he had sent his own lawyer down there to make sure there was nothing to obscure his title to the land. Evidently Tarant had found this part of the *derrotero* among the papers. But this was only a third of it. Where was the rest of it? The light grew brighter. So this was why Rockland had sent for him. He thought that he, Crawford, knew about the map—knew, perhaps, who held the missing pieces. Santa Anna's chests, Rockland had said, Santa Anna's chests. All at once he found himself muttering the words aloud, "Santa Anna's chests—"

As though the words were a magic Sesame, Rockland opened his eyes. Drawing on some hidden reservoir of strength, he pulled himself to a sitting position. "Where's the rest of it, Glenn?" he gasped. "Does Delcazar know? Glenn, Glenn, where's the rest—"

Crawford caught at the man as Rockland sank back. "Otis?"

It was the muted footsteps, then, coming across the Brussels carpet in the outer room. Crawford had allowed Rockland to drop back when Ed Kenmare's bulk filled the doorway. A vague pain moved over the sheriff's heavy weathered features.

"The manager heard a ruckus up here," he said. "I guess he was right. No, Glenn—"

"Yes, Ed," said Glenn, violently, scooping up his Henry and whirling back toward the man. Kenmare had his own six-shooter only half out of its holster. He stopped that way, staring at the .44. There were other men behind the sheriff now, several of the cowmen from the patio and lobby, the hotel manager in a white morning coat.

"I guess there's no use denying it, is there?" said Crawford, through his teeth.

Kenmare let his eyes drop to the Henry's wooden butt. Crawford felt it then, sticky against his fingers, and realized the wood must have been lying in the blood from Rockland's head. A nausea swept him.

"Ed," he said, unable to keep from it, "I didn't, I didn't—"

His bitter voice trailed off as he saw resignation in Kenmare's faded eyes. "Listen, son," the man told him. "It won't do you no good this way. Give me that gun now."

"No." The finger lever made a sharp click, cocking, and with his hand holding it down, Crawford started backing toward the window. "Think I'd have a chance? It's all here, isn't it? All right here, cinched up tighter'n a bucking rig. No loose lashings even. Everything to hang me. I'm not going to be taken for that, Ed."

"Glenn," said Kenmare, with that same weighty reluctance, "for once, don't be a hothead. You go off half-cocked like this and bugger your bronc every time. This just won't do you any good—"

"Don't do it, Jason," Crawford shouted, turning his gun toward one of the cattlemen behind Kenmare. Harry Jason stopped trying to shift back of Kenmare where Crawford wouldn't see him draw his gun, and moved his hand carefully away from the wooden butt of the weapon. There was no intelligent reasoning in Crawford now. Only a terrible consciousness of that dead body on the floor, and a blind, animal urge to escape this. He lifted his leg over the iron railing of the balcony onto the ledge outside. There was the first violent movement among the men in the room as he crouched down to drop off the ledge, and he heard someone shout. Then he jumped.

It was not a long fall, and he broke it by catching the edge of the balcony with his free hand and hanging there till his arm was stretched out with his weight, then letting go. One of his high heels turned under him as he struck the flagstones below, and he let himself go down on his knees and then roll it off to keep from spraining an ankle. As he leaped to his feet, Kenmare appeared on the balcony, gun out. Crawford was already running toward the front entrance, past the line of cane chairs. There were still half a dozen cattlemen sitting there, and two of them were standing at the end, and Kenmare was apparently fearful of hitting them if he shot.

"Stop him," shouted the lawman. "Crawford. He killed Rockland. Get him, you fools—"

The men standing made an abortive shift to block Crawford's passage, but he was already opposite them, and surprise held the other men in their chairs till he was almost to the door. He saw several pulling at their guns, but Mexicans and cowhands were passing by outside in the street, or stopping farther beyond in the Plaza to gape curiously, and a bullet might have struck one of them. There were half a dozen cow ponies at a cottonwood rack in front of the Manger, and as Crawford reached them he noticed that the reins of the first were tied in a hitch that could be knocked free. He did it with the tip of his gun, throwing the ribbons over the animal's neck. Excited by Crawford's running up like that, the hairy little black started to whirl inward. Crawford jumped for the stirrup with one foot, letting the centrifugal force slap him into the saddle as the horse whirled on around.

"Hey," shouted one of the cattlemen, streaming out of the patio behind him. "Get off that horse, Crawford, he's mine—"

But Crawford was already turning the animal into Blum Street. Halfway down the block he cut through an alley onto Commerce and turned at the corner of Commerce and Alamo, wheeling into another alley that led directly down to the river. He crashed through a line of washing hung behind a squalid Mexican hovel and scattered a bunch of cackling hens, tearing a white *camisa* off his head, his hat going with it. A Mexican woman ran from the hut, waving her arms and squealing at him, and behind that he could hear the dim sounds of running horses. He had gone down Blum to make them think he was heading west out of town, and hoped they would not discover his true direction till he had left by the south. He slid the pony down the stone coping banking the river, letting the current carry him beneath the Market Street bridge before trying to reach the opposite bank. He got out of town following back alleys and side streets, and then broke into South Flores Street. And now, as he pushed the laboring pony toward the twin spires of Mission Concepción, it began to come.

There had been no room for it in the violent excitement of those first few minutes, with all his concentration on escape. But now, with the steady beat of running hoofs beneath him, it began to grow in him. First, perhaps, it was a consciousness of that steady shuddering pound of hoofs beneath him. Then, the constant, heated movement of the horse's muscles, the dim sense of its flanks, rising and falling with the heavy breathing, the feel of its shoulders beneath the saddle moving back and forth. And finally, more than the movement and the sound outside him. Something within. He did not know where it started. In his legs, perhaps. Or his groin. Somewhere down there. A strange, thin, hollow sensation.

"No—"

He didn't know whether it had been in his mind or whether he had said it. He turned in the saddle, staring down the road behind, trying to blot it from his consciousness. He was past the fields of white niggerheads about Concepción, and was approaching the second mission, San José de Aguayo, which had been established by the Spaniards here in 1720. But it was growing in him. He was sweating beneath the armpits now. It was recognizable now. Pain. More than that—hollow, nebulous sickness at the pit of his stomach. Pain. Pinpricks of it, shooting up his legs. A hoarse, strained sob escaped him. How could it be? They had told him, no. He was healed. How can it be? *I'm healed, damn you, I'm healed.*

The roof of San Aguayo had fallen in, and only a few windows were left in the south wall, protected by the remains of delicate iron *rejas,* their tarnished panes flashing dully in the sun as Crawford passed by. He was barely conscious of this. He was sweating now, his fists gripping the reins so desperately the knuckles gleamed translucently through the skin. The pain seemed to have sound now. His head was roaring with it. He was shaking violently now, and the horse felt it and began reflecting his lack of control, breaking its stride, shifting from side to side down the road.

The stepped belfries of San Francisco de la Espade rose into view. The last ruins of the *baluarte* built for the defense of the mission ran parallel to the road, sections of this bastion crumbling off into the ruts of the highway. The horse changed leads to side-step some of the adobe fallen onto the road, and Crawford lurched out of the saddle, barely recovering himself. He heard someone making hoarse, guttural sounds, and realized it was himself. And now, more than the pain, something else was rising in him. The hot, sweaty fetor of the horse filled him with a violent nausea. He had a wild impulse to escape it. He caught himself actually stiffening up to throw himself free of the running horse.

"No!"

Again, he did not know if it was in his head, or if he had shouted it. The very sound of the running horse seemed to fill his brain now. Each thundering hoofbeat was a separate note of agony. And more than the agony which filled him, that other something he could not define, or would not, so confused with the pain now he could not tell the two apart. Finally he could stand it no longer. Brutally, he reined in the horse. The animal brought himself to a series of stiff-legged halts that almost jolted him over its head. He swung off the lathered, heaving animal, and then, standing with his face toward its hairy wet hide, he was filled with that nausea again. He wheeled away from the horse, stumbling across the road to a pile of rubble that marked the remains of the aqueduct. With a hoarse exhalation, he lowered himself weakly to the adobe, dropping his head forward into his hands, so that the black hair fell through his grimy fingers in dank, sweaty tendrils.

"I *can* ride," he said aloud, in a desperate voice, "I *can* ride!"

Chapter Two

SANTA ANNA'S CHESTS

IT HAD A MILLION FACES. At dawn it was a dim, foggy mask. At noon it leered in brassy, burning malignance. At night it was a cunning visage, sometimes filled with bizarre mutations by the caprice of moonlight, sometimes cloaked in the unrelieved sin of utter blackness. This was the *brasada*.

Glenn Crawford did not know how many weeks of weary travel lay behind him since he had left that cow pony by the mission and had struck out on foot for this borderland which had provided sanctuary for so many fugitives. Now, crouched in a thicket of black chaparral, with the late afternoon sun falling through the branches to cast a weird shadow pattern across his back, Crawford was filled with an oppressive sense of its infinite mystery. It was a Spanish word, *brasada,* and there was no English equivalent. For it was not brushland in the ordinary sense. Not scattered clumps of mesquite dotting an arid prairie, or small thickets of sage in a sandy plain. It was a jungle. A dry jungle, as vast and unexplored as the Amazon jungles, stretching through southern Texas between the Nueces River and the Rio Grande for uncounted miles, in many places so thick as to be impossible of penetration.

Until he had reached its safety, Crawford's primary instinct had been the simple animal urge of escape. But once within its borders, a desire to get at the root of this thing, and to clear himself, began to grow in him. And though he knew the dangers involved, it had inevitably drawn him to the Big O, where the whole thing had started.

Otis Rockland's father had established the spread here in the *brasada* just before the Texas Revolution, shipping lumber for his house from New Orleans. It was a strange building, in a land where most structures were low adobe hovels. Its two stories rose gaunt and lonely against the dark horizon of brush, the flat gambrel roof supporting a pair of glassed-in cupolas over the front. Crawford had been here since noon, watching it, not yet knowing what he had meant to do when he reached the spread. The sun had burned bronze streaks through his shaggy mane of black hair, and a scrubby, matted beard grew up into the hungry hollows beneath his high cheekbones, rendering his face gaunt and wolfish. His whole body jerked with the sudden crackle of brush behind him, and he started to whirl and rise from his hunkers and pull his gun around all in the same violent movement.

"Never mind, Glenn, you'd never do it in time," said the man standing there. He waited a moment, grinning, and then spoke again with a deliberate, slow irony. "If you'll drop that Henry, we'll be able to talk comfortably."

Crawford let the rifle slip reluctantly from stiff fingers, and then straightened his legs out until he was standing, faced toward the man they called Cabezablanca for his head of pure white hair. His face was as smooth and unlined as a coffee bean, and he wore a pair of tight buckskin leggings they called *chivarras* this near the border, and a blue cotton shirt, and Crawford had never seen him without the Winchester he carried now.

"It's been a long time since you busted broncs for the Big O, Glenn," said Cabezablanca. "Ain't you going to say something? *Buenos días,* for an old *amigo,* or how are things?" He waited a moment, the smile slipping from his thin, beardless lips. "You better be civil to me, Glenn. I'm a very dangerous man." He halted again, and when he realized Crawford would not answer, a sullen anger tightened his lips. "Very well, let us go and see what they want to do with you."

Crawford turned around, moving from the screen of brush in stiff, catty steps, the tense forward thrust of his shoulders giving them that narrow appearance. He was aware that Cabezablanca stooped to pick up the Henry as he followed. Crawford had been watching the crew working a bunch of horses in the corrals, and now, as he drew near, he saw that they had pulled a new animal into the tight chute between the smaller pen where the animals were held and the larger one where they were worked. It was a big black animal the Mexicans called a *puro negro,* throwing itself crazily against the bars of the chute, the whole structure shuddering with its violent struggles. Crawford was not aware that he had stopped till Cabezablanca came up beside him.

"Yeah, Crawford," said the white-headed man, watching him narrowly. "Africano. Sort of brings back things, doesn't it? That black devil's still rolling them, and nobody's broke it yet."

A man threw a dally rope over the top of the chute, noosing the black animal's neck and pulling it tight against the bars. The beast fought wildly a moment, banging its skull against the cedar poles. The corrals shook again, and yellow dust rose about that section, obscuring the horse. When the dust settled, the *puro negro* had quit battling, and stood with its forelegs stiff, breathing heavily through its nose. A tall, slat-limbed Mexican climbed to the top of the chute, and the men below handed him up a double-rigged Porter. He dropped the heavy saddle on the horse, and a man below reached through the bars to get the front girth, pulling the latigo through the cinch rings and yanking the girth tight. Africano squealed shrilly, trying to jerk away again. Then another Mexican climbed up the bars of the chute and stood at the top, pulling his belt up.

He was so broad he appeared short, his close-cropped hair beginning to gray at the temples. His great shoulders bunched like sides of beef beneath the strained wool of a faded *charro* jacket with a few tattered remnants of what might have been gold embroidery on its lapels. He wore a pair of tight rawhide leggings, and the rolling muscles of his thighs had burst the seams in several places between hip and knee.

Crawford licked dry lips. "Who is it?"

"Quartel," said Cabezablanca. "When you killed Rockland in San Antonio, a lot of the Big O crew drifted. Bueno Bailey and me are about the only ones left of the old bunch. Rockland didn't have no heirs. So his lawyer was given the job of cleaning up the estate. There's a lot of cattle to be choused out of that brush and Tarant had to get a new ramrod. And Quartel's him."

"But—" Crawford moved his hand vaguely toward the horse—"Africano—"

"The nigger sort of fascinates Quartel, I guess," grinned the other. "He's been trying to break it ever since he got here. That black devil almost stove him up a couple of times."

Quartel was straddling the bars of the chute with his feet, leaning down to tug at the saddle a couple of times and test the cinches. They finally got the bit in and pulled the rawhide reins up to where Quartel could take hold of them. He waved his free hand, and the man below pulled out the drop bar which held the door of the chute closed. Then they untied the rope from the black's neck and swung open the door. As the beast lunged forward, Quartel dropped into the saddle.

Africano was larger than most brush horses, though not any taller, standing maybe fifteen hands, with a prodigiously muscled rump that indicated more than a little quarter blood, and a savage, vicious action to its every movement. The animal boiled over almost before it had left the chute. Quartel had not found his right stirrup as the beast erupted, but by the time Africano hit the top of its first buck, the man's foot was in the oxbow, and when the black stiff-legged down into the ground, Quartel was set for it.

Even then, his broad, heavy body trembled to the awful jar of it. Crawford's face twisted, and his hands were gripping the bars of the corral with a strange desperation.

The black raced down the corral with a high, collected action and then stopped abruptly with its forelegs jamming the ground like ramrods, pinwheeling in its own billow of dust. It was all balance with Quartel. Crawford did not think he had ever seen such a relaxed seat on a bucker. The man shifted his weight back and forth almost delicately, gauging each violent movement of the horse to perfection.

"There it goes," said Cabezablanca.

Crawford rose up on his toes against the bars. Africano had started to roll. Quartel stepped off with an incredibly lithe movement for his heavy body, as the horse went down. The black rolled completely over, and Quartel was there ready to swing onto its back again as the animal came up, jamming his feet into the stirrups and raking the animal's dusty, lathered flanks with great Mexican cart-wheel spurs. The black screamed in a frenzied, crazy way as it realized the man was still on its back. With a shrill whinny, it began rolling again, madly, cleverly, devilishly, watching Quartel out of its glassy eyes, heavy chest briny with lather. Crawford watched with a terrible fascination, unaware of how tightly he was hanging onto the bars or how loud and harsh his heavy, labored breathing was.

On its fourth roll, Africano twisted while still on its back and switched ends before coming up, kicking at Quartel with its hind feet. Quartel dodged the kick,

shouting something, and slapped the animal's rump to
come up over the legs as they struck the ground, hitting the saddle with a jar that drew a gasp from Crawford. Africano raced forward, halted abruptly, pivoted
on one hind foot. Quartel was thrown off balance by
the spin, and while his weight was still on the off side,
the black reared up and fell back deliberately. Quartel
had to kick free and jump to keep from being mashed
beneath twelve hundred pounds of vicious black demon,
and he lost control completely.

The animal came up with a triumphant whinny, whirling toward Quartel. The dust billowed up about the dim
shouting movement filling the corral then, and Crawford
could see only dimly what happened. A red-bearded hand
was galloping in on one of the cutting horses to try and
reach the black before it trampled Quartel. But the rider
spun the big loop over his head once before throwing it,
and the wily black saw it coming and wheeled away.

"Damn you, Innes, why don't you go back to snag-
ging fence posts," shouted Quartel, stumbling to his
feet and lurching for the rope. He caught that end and
jerked it violently, almost unhorsing Innes as the rope
was torn from his hands. Then Quartel whirled around,
snaking in the rope with quick, skillful flirts until he
had the other end. The red-bearded rider had wheeled
and was trying to run into Africano broadside now to
force it away from Quartel. But Africano leaped ahead,
dodging the man, and wheeled toward Quartel again,
that maniacal intent plain in its bloodshot eyes. "Get
out of the way," Quartel roared hoarsely at Innes. "I
swear you don't know any more about handling horses
than a woman. Get out of the way—"

The Mexicans called it a *mangana*, and not many
men could have done it in such a position. The black
horse had outmaneuvered Innes, and was racing a dead
run at Quartel. Quartel stood there with the rope in

both hands, not even spinning it, a confident grin on his face. When the black was so near it looked certain to run Quartel down, the man made his toss. It was a California throw, down low without a spin so the horse could not spot it until the loop was actually in the air. Quartel snapped the rope behind him at his hip, then dragged it forward with a swift flirt of his wrist, hand pointed down and the loop swinging out so that it practically stood on edge. It was timed perfectly. Quartel took one step away like a bullfighter, and the *puro negro* thundered past him, so close its lathered shoulder twitched his *charro* jacket, and ran headlong into that loop standing there. Quartel turned away with the rope across his hip, and his thick body jerked hard as the horse snapped the rope taut and fell headlong. Then he casually dropped the rope to the ground and walked away, while other hands ran in with the short tie ropes they called peales, to hog-tie the vicious beast while it was still down.

Crawford realized only then how his fingers ached. He released them from the cedar-post bar. His shirt was sticking to his back with sweat, and he heard that heavy, labored breathing. Him? And something else. The same thing he had known on that cow pony up by San Antonio. Not pain exactly, though there were those little spasms twitching at his legs. But something more insidious than that, down in his belly somewhere, a thin, nauseating consciousness. His eyes went to the black horse, still kicking and squealing as they hog-tied it within the corral, and a new wave of it swept him. He turned away, clenching his teeth, trying to drown it with anger. Then he became aware of how Cabezablanca was looking at him.

"What's the matter, Crawford? You look like it was you riding the African instead of Quartel." The white-headed man waited, that sly grin fading as he saw Crawford was not going to speak. He indicated the house,

finally, with the tip of his Winchester. "Let's go. Maybe
Huerta will want to see you."

"But I've already seen him," said a heavy, jaded voice
from behind them. "I've been watching him for some
time now."

The overdrapes of green striped satin had been pulled
aside from the front windows of the dining-room to let
the last shafts of afternoon sunlight cross the dark
Empire Aubusson and gleam brazenly on the brass-
headed nails which studded the green morocco upholster-
ing of the chairs. The man who had stood behind Crawford and Cabezablanca at the corrals was Doctor Feliz
Huerta, and he followed Crawford into the dining-room
now.

Crawford did not think he had ever seen such infinite
dissolution in a face. The minute pattern of blood vessels
was faintly visible in Huerta's heavy lids, giving them
a bluish cast. His eyes, when they were visible behind
these lids, held a dull, jaded lackluster in their black
pupils, and his flesh was smooth and soft-looking, lined
about the mouth and eyes like an old satchel. His black
hair was parted in the middle, graying at the temples
and receding there to form a peak down his forehead
which, added to the strong arch of his brows, gave his
features a satanic cast.

"You may go now, Whitehead," he said.

Cabezablanca shifted uncomfortably. "Listen, you
don't seem to understand. This is Glenn Crawford—"

It seemed to cause Huerta infinite effort to turn toward the man. For a moment, their eyes met. Whitehead's
mouth was still open from his words, and he drew a small,
surprised breath through it. Then he began to back out
of the room.

Huerta moved his glance around to Crawford when
Cabezablanca had left. "They say he is a very dangerous

man," he murmured, moving languidly to the old English sideboard. Lifting one of the brass rings on the top drawer, he pulled it open, taking a silver plate out and putting it on top. There was a small pile of reddish beans, and he selected one from this, popping it into his mouth. "You'll excuse me. An old complaint."

Crawford could retain it no longer. "What kind of horse you on?"

Huerta's face revealed some small surprise. "I thought you might like to have dinner with us. Jacinto will bring it in a few moments."

"No," said Crawford, moving his hand viciously. "Something else. What is it, Huerta? What are you doing here?"

One of Huerta's sardonic black brows lifted quizzically. "You are such a suspicious man, Crawford. I have known Otis Rockland for some time. He invited me to visit him. I arrived to find him murdered in San Antonio. It was quite a shock. Ah—" his glance had passed Crawford and was focused on the doorway—"Merida, Wallace, I'm glad you've come. We have a dinner guest."

Crawford turned around. Wallace Tarant had been Otis Rockland's lawyer a long time, and Crawford knew him well enough. But it was the woman who commanded his attention. Her beauty struck him with such an impact that he felt a distinct physical reaction pass through his body. Not many women could have worn their hair in such a severe coif without detracting from their allure. It was so black it looked blue, parted in the center and drawn back to a shimmering bun at the nape of her neck. It gave accent to the faintly exotic planes of her face. Her only jewelry was a large cabochon emerald in an onyx brooch that rode the mature swell of her breasts just below the low-cut top of her black silk dress.

Her slightly oblique eyes held a candid interest, meeting his. The blood thickened in his throat. A vague irritation swept Crawford that she should affect him so strongly.

"This is Merida Lopez, Crawford," said Huerta. "She came with me from Mexico City."

"Crawford." It escaped her on a throaty breath, and those large black eyes took in the tense line of his body, and a faint smile stirred her rich lips. "I imagined you, somewhat—like this."

Wallace Tarant took a step that placed him at the woman's side. He had a broad-shouldered, narrow-hipped frame that looked good in his tailored town coat. His face, with its square brow and wide, thin-lipped mouth, should have held a palpable strength. But his eyes would not meet Crawford's. His voice was small for such a large man.

"What's the idea, Huerta?" he said.

"Whitehead found him in the brush watching the house," said Huerta. "I thought perhaps we might like a little talk with him. You, as Rockland's lawyer, should appreciate the value of that."

"Isn't it a little dangerous," said Tarant.

"I think Crawford knows how little chance there is of escape," said Huerta. "By whatever door a man leaves this house, he has to cross several hundred yards of open compound before reaching the protection of the brush. At the present moment, there are half a dozen men out there, just waiting for the chance. As for his presence among us, you aren't afraid of him, are you, Wallace?"

Tarant flushed, moved stiffly to pull out a chair for Merida. Crawford could not tell if it was deliberate, but in passing him the woman's body touched his hip. His whole frame stiffened with the momentary, warm, silken pressure, and he could not help the sharp breath he drew. Then she was by, and he saw the faint, ironic smile twitch at Huerta's lips. Crawford turned angrily toward the table, but before he could reach a chair, the whole room

began to tremble. He knew who was coming before the
man appeared. Jacinto del Rio had cooked for the Rock-
lands as long as anyone in the brush could remember.
The three dominating factors of his life were apparent
enough as he rumbled into the doorway from the entrance hall. His prodigious belly was a remarkable edifice
to *tortillas* and frijoles. The blue network of broken
veins patterning his flushed jowls indicated a singular
capacity for tequila and pulque. The reluctance of his
every movement reflected his veritable passion for the
national pastime of siesta. He held a great silver tureen
of soup on a tray high before his face, and it prevented
him from seeing Crawford at first.

"*Trabajo, trabajo*," he grumbled, "always work. First
it's breakfast in the bunkhouse. 'Hyacinth cook some
more eggs.' 'Hyacinth this coffee tastes like alkali.' Hyacinth this, Hyacinth that. Then breakfast for the big
house. 'Hyacinth you're late.' 'Hyacinth you didn't put
enough clabber in the biscuits.' Hyacinth this, Hyacinth
that. Me, who was made for nothing but wassail and song
and laughter, sweating like an *esclavo* all my life. You
know what my father he tell me?"

"Yes, yes," said Huerta wearily. "If you don't set that
tray down soon we'll be eating breakfast instead of
dinner."

"He tell me, 'Hyacinth, there are two sins in the world
—working and fighting, working and fighting—and if
you avoid both of them, you will surely go to heaven.'"
Jacinto set the tray down, his eyes rolling upward in a
fat face. "*Por Dios!* it looks like I'll never get there now.
My poor *padre* must be turning over in his grave to see
how I have desecrated his wishes. To think of me, little
Hyacinth of the River, meant for nothing but—"

His eyes had focused on Crawford for the first time,
and his words ended in a bleat. He held up a fat hand,
trying to say something, but nothing would come out.

He turned toward Huerta, sweat rolling down his face with his effort to speak. He whirled back to Crawford, his whole body twitching. Then he looked to Huerta again.

"*Por Dios!*" he croaked. "Doctor. Please. Crawford. That's him. I was born for laughter and wassail and song. You aren't going to do anything. How did he get here? No *violencia*. Please. My delicate sensibilities would revolt. You won't—"

"My dear Hyacinth," said Huerta. "There won't, I assure you, be any violence. Now please go and bring the rest of the meal." Jacinto backed out of the room, sputtering, and Huerta's sardonic glance slipped around to Crawford. "Won't you sit down? You make me nervous."

Crawford moved across to pull out a chair across from the woman, feeling her eyes on him, and lowered his tense body onto the green morocco leather. They were all watching him now.

"Would you serve, Wallace?" said Huerta, leaning back in his chair. He surveyed Crawford for a moment. "You know," he said finally, "most people think your motive for killing Otis Rockland was revenge. But somehow, that doesn't satisfy us."

"Doesn't it?" said Crawford.

The woman's laugh was as throaty as her voice. It caused his glance to shift to her face with a jerk. She sat there with that smile, making no effort to explain her amusement. It drew a reasonless anger from him. He gripped his knees with his hands, beneath the linen cloth.

"Did you ever hear the story of Santa Anna's chests, Mr. Crawford?" Merida Lopez asked, finally, a strange, obscure mockery coloring her voice.

"No," answered Crawford stiffly.

She tasted her soup, eyes still on him. "In April of 1826, at the close of the Texas Revolution, General Santa Anna had led his Mexican army halfway across

Texas after General Houston's forces, finally catching
him at San Jacinto. There were two major political
parties in Mexico at that time, the Federalists and the
Centralists. The Centralists had been trying for some
time to break Santa Anna's growing power in politics.
For four or five months they had managed to have the
army pay withheld, but Santa Anna finally got a pay
train sent from Mexico City. The battle of San Jacinto
was in progress when this mule train arrived, and a
party of Texans cut it off before it could reach the
Mexican army, chasing it westward into the brush somewhere south of the Nueces. The Texans finally caught
the Mexicans, and in the battle that followed the greater
part of the Mexicans were killed. But the mules had
disappeared. They have not been found since."

"Neither has the Lost Nigger Mine, or Steinheimer's
millions," said Crawford. "I been listening to windies
like that since I was a button."

"Ah, a skeptic." Again that mockery, more palpable
this time. She toyed with her soupspoon. The faint movement of her wrist drew his glance, and he found himself
wondering how the soft white skin would feel. "And still,
Crawford, doesn't it intrigue you?" Her voice penetrated
his attention, and he raised his gaze self-consciously. Just
her hand. Just the movement of her hand like that. What
the hell? "Five months' pay for an army, Crawford. Does
a man like you have any conception of that kind of
money? Men would kill for it. Even governments. And
there is more than just the story. There is what the Mexicans call a *derrotero.*"

She let her eyes lift momentarily from the spoon, but
he had kept his face carefully blank. He was beginning
to notice her enunciation now. The accent was discernible sometimes. Her careful precision seemed an effort
to hide it.

"This *derrotero*," she said. "Literally a map, a chart.

It was made by the captain of the mule train. When he realized the Texans would inevitably catch him, he secreted the pay chests somewhere in the brush, making the chart. Fearing that, if he entrusted the whole of the chart to one man, that man might be captured, he divided it into three portions. Thus, if one or even two of the men were caught, the chests would still be safe, for the hiding place could not be located without all three portions. One section he sent with an Indian to Santa Anna himself at San Jacinto. The second part he gave to his lieutenant, to carry to the Federalists in Mexico City. The third he kept himself."

"Yeah?" said Crawford.

"Yes," she said, smiling in dim amusement at his acrid reticence. For a moment, her eyes were half-closed, studying him, and they held a slumberous, provocative temptation. It stirred something primal within him. He had felt it before. But not this way. Not just looking in a woman's eyes.

"The captain of that mule train was the uncle of your friend Pio Delcazar!"

It went through him with a palpable shock, and it was not till after she had finished speaking that Crawford realized what she had been doing, with those eyes. They had turned hard and speculative, now, and with the spell broken, Crawford felt the twisted expression her words had drawn to his face. He tried to regain that inscrutability, but knew it was too late. There was a certain triumphant satisfaction in the way Merida allowed her gaze to drop to the table as she began eating the soup again. And now the two men were watching him. He felt the sweat break out on his palms.

"*Carne adobada, carne adobada?*" said Jacinto, waddling in. "You don't know how long I pickled it in brine. I fry the spices and chile till the juices stream out of the pork, and—" he trailed off, seeing how they were all watching Crawford. He turned to Huerta, wringing his fingers. "Doctor, please, I beseech you—"

"The coffee, Hyacinth, the coffee," murmured Huerta, waving a languid hand at the cook without looking away from Crawford.

Jacinto almost choked on the breath he took, and backed out, staring wide-eyed at Crawford. "*Sí*. The *café*. *Sí*."

Tarant began to serve the meat dish Jacinto had brought. "When you had that ruckus with Rockland in the living-room here, Bueno Bailey said it was over Delcazar," he said.

"You know what it was over," said Crawford. "You got Del's land for Rockland that way."

Huerta leaned forward slightly. "Was it just the land?"

"Del's my *compadre*," said Crawford. "You're Mexican. You know what the word is."

"Crawford," said Huerta, bending farther forward, "we should, of course, send you back to San Antonio. But there are other things which could be done."

"You're riding a muddy creek."

"A colloquialism," murmured the woman. "How quaint."

Crawford's narrow, dark head turned toward her with an angry jerk. She was watching him from beneath her brows in that mocking way, chin tucked in, and it formed a small crease in the rich flesh beneath her jaw. There was something concupiscent about it.

"We think your quarrel with Rockland was over more than the way he acquired Delcazar's land," said Huerta.

Crawford found it difficult to take his eyes off Merida. "Do you?"

"Oh, Huerta," the woman muttered petulantly, "can't you see you'll never get anywhere beating about the bush with him—"

"You'll never get anywhere with him anyway," said

Wallace Tarant. "I know Glenn Crawford, Huerta. We'd better send him back to San Antonio right now."

"Oh, no," said Huerta, leaning back. "Not at all. I think if we kept him here long enough, we would find a way of convincing him that it is to his advantage to—ah—" he moved his hand, as if seeking the word—"co-operate, with us. Yes. Co-operate. Don't you, Merida?"

The woman's laugh held a husky sensuality. "Perhaps. Even if not—it would be interesting."

Wallace Tarant put down his fork angrily. "Don't be a fool, Huerta. Having Crawford here is like sitting on a keg of powder with a lighted match. What would Kenmare do if he found we'd caught Crawford and hadn't notified the authorities?"

"Kenmare won't find out," said Huerta, turning toward the man, "unless someone tells him. Ah, our coffee."

Jacinto set the urn down hesitantly, glaring about at them. He started to speak, then caught Huerta's eye, and backed out of the room, muttering to himself. Smiling faintly, Huerta indicated that Tarant should pour. Then he held out a cup.

"Mexican style, Crawford. Perhaps you'll like it. Boiled in milk and water and sweetened in the pot with *poloncillo,* our brown sugar. I was surprised to find how few of the hands here drank it like this. I know Quartel sweetens it with molasses sometimes." His eyes dropped to his own cup, and he stirred it absently. "Speaking of Quartel, that was quite an exhibition this afternoon, wasn't it? I don't think I've ever seen such a vicious horse. And what a magnificent beast a man would have if he could break it." He looked up abruptly. "Oh, excuse me, Crawford, I—" he moved his hand in an apologetic gesture—"I wasn't thinking—"

The woman frowned at him. "Hm?"

"The horse," said Huerta, looking at Merida, "the

horse."

"What about the horse?" she said.

"I don't mean that," said Huerta. "I—"

"Never mind," said Crawford. "My legs are all right."

"Oh?" Huerta's arched brows rose. "I got a different impression. You weren't riding."

"I lost my horse on the Flores Road."

"It was hit?"

"I lost it, that's all," said Crawford.

"Oh." Huerta took out a jade cigarette holder, fitting a smoke into it. He leaned back, looking at Crawford. "You were watching Africano out in the corral, that way."

"What about the way I was watching it?"

Huerta's eyes dropped meditatively to the coffee cup, and he allowed twin streamers of smoke to leave his nostrils. "I guess I got the wrong impression, Crawford. You'll have to pardon me."

"Impression about what, Huerta?" said Tarant.

Huerta seemed to rouse himself with an effort. "Ah, nothing. Nothing, Tarant. You're not drinking your coffee, Crawford. Is it too sweet for you? Pour him another cup, Tarant." The woman was watching him narrowly now, and Huerta let his eyes meet hers momentarily before he leaned forward to put his elbows on the table. He took a sip of his own coffee, looking down the middle of the table in that meditation again. "They say a man is getting old when he starts reminiscing, but I can't help being reminded of an instance I ran across in Monterrey some years ago. After the war I chanced to be employed by a Mexican firm with interests in a mine north of the city. I had been company doctor some months when one of the lower shafts caved in, killing half a dozen of the men. I managed to patch up most of those who escaped with minor injuries. There was one miner, a huge giant of a fellow, whose legs had been crushed somewhat beneath the slide. My operations were singularly successful, and within five or six months he was as good as new, the bones knit perfectly and the muscles gave no sign of the damage. During his convalescence, there had been no pain. Yet, the very first day he went back to work, he experienced the most acute agony in his legs."

The little muscles jumped out all along Crawford's jaw suddenly. Huerta looked up, smiled faintly. "Yes— the most acute agony. I could find nothing organically wrong with him, absolutely nothing. In my office, he did not feel the pain. I took him back to the mine. As he approached the mouth of the shaft in which he had worked, the agony returned. All the symptoms of genuine pain. Sweating, trembling, tears in the eyes. I could not account for it. There was utterly no reason for him to feel the pain. I administered drugs, enough to deaden the greatest agony. It had no effect. Then I took him away from the mine. As soon as it was out of sight, the pain receded, disappeared."

Merida's face had lifted as he spoke, a tight furrow appearing between her brows. "You mean—his mind—"

"*Sí,*" said Huerta. He was adjusting a fresh cigarette carefully in its holder. "I came to that conclusion finally. The mind plays funny tricks on us sometimes. That cave-in had been such a ghastly experience that he actually felt pain when he returned to the scene. And worse than the pain. Fear. He could never work at his trade again; he could never get near a mine without feeling that pain. And that fear. He tried to fight it. He had been a brave man once. He tried to force himself back into the mines. But in the shaft he became a sniveling, gibbering coward, crying and puking like a baby, unable to speak coherently even. Yes, the mind does play funny tricks on us—" Huerta held his cigarette holder out abruptly. "Crawford, you've spilled your coffee!"

Chapter Three

HUERTA WAS RIGHT!

THE BUNKHOUSE AND COOKSHACK stood a few hundred
yards south of the house, two adobe structures connected
by a covered dog-run. Rockland's father had put them up
to live in while his large dwelling was being built, con-
structing their walls not with mud bricks but by the
older Indian method of making forms out of willow
shoots and cotton sheeting, pouring the mud into these
forms, and peeling off the cotton after the adobe had
dried. Unless these walls were replastered every six
months or so, they began to crack, and the inside of
the cookshack was already beginning to show a network
of minute fissures across its whitewashed surface. It was
here Crawford had spent the night, an oppressive sense
of the hostility which surrounded him keeping him from
much sleep. After breakfast, all the crew had left the
bunkhouse but Bueno Bailey.

He was gaunt as an alley cat, and he parted his long
yellow hair in the middle and slicked it down with bacon
grease, and he sat in the stifling morning heat of the
shack, idly spinning the cylinder of his six-shooter.

"Will you stop that, Bueno?" snapped Crawford.

Bailey looked up at Crawford, who had been standing against the doorpost, staring outside. "I've seen cattle
look out between the bars of a pen that same way,
Glenn," he said, putting his long forefinger against the
cylinder of his gun to give it another, deliberate whirl.
"You don't need to get ideas. Why do you think they
left me here?"

"I'll bite," said Crawford. "Why?"

"They haven't decided what to do with you yet,"

murmured Bailey. "Tarant was for taking you right back to San Antonio, but Huerta didn't want that, for some reason. Either way, it's a cinch they don't want you to get away. *Sabe?*"

"What's Huerta got to say about it?" said Crawford.

"He's some friend of Rockland's," Bueno told him.

"That doesn't seem to me enough reason for the way he assumes authority around here," Crawford muttered. "I thought Quartel was the ramrod."

"There's some kind of deal between Huerta and Tarant," Bailey answered, giving the cylinder another spin. "Quartel's tried to buck Huerta a couple of times and Tarant stood behind the doctor. Quartel almost lost his job the second time. Tarant gave us the idea we'd better do what Huerta liked if we wanted to keep on working here."

Crawford glanced at the gun. "I asked you to stop that."

Bueno leaned forward on the three-legged stool, placing his elbows on his knees to look up at Crawford. "So you had to come back, Glenn," he said. "Why?"

"Maybe I came back to pay a few debts," said Crawford thinly.

The oily click of the cylinder stopped abruptly. "You owe somebody something?"

"Still snipping cinches, Bueno?"

The stool crashed to the floor, and Crawford whirled from where he had been standing in the doorway to meet Bailey as the man came up against him. The only thing that prevented their bodies from meeting was the gun Bailey held against Crawford's body. The man's milky eyes were slitted, and the smell of that bacon grease in his hair nauseated Crawford.

"Chew that a little finer," said Bueno, through his teeth.

"Africano never could have rolled me under if that

rigging hadn't come apart," Crawford said thinly. "I saw the cinch on that saddle afterward. It hadn't pulled loose by itself."

"Glenn—" Bailey let it out on a hissing breath—"I think you better change your mind about that."

"I know who did Rockland's stable jobs for him," said Crawford.

The gun dug into his belly. "Glenn—"

"Yes?" said Crawford. "Make it a better job than that first time, Bueno."

Bueno stood there a moment longer, his breath hot and fetid against Crawford's face. Then his weight settled back onto his heels. He turned around and set the stool upright and lowered himself onto it once more. He began twirling the cylinder again with his forefinger. Crawford saw it tremble against the blued steel.

"When the time comes, Crawford," said Bueno, not looking up, "I will make it a better job, you can depend on that. I'll finish the job."

The harsh laugh from the doorway caused Crawford to turn back that way. He wondered how long Quartel had stood there. The man moved on into the room, a pawky smile on his sensuous lips. The pores of his cheeks and nostrils were large enough to be clearly discernible, and they exuded a heavy sweat, lending a greasy look to the thick brown flesh of his face. He stuck his thumbs in the waistband of his dirty *chivarras,* leaning back slightly.

"It seems that you haven't got one friend left on the Rockland *estancia,* doesn't it, *Señor* Crawford?" he said.

"En la cárcel y en la cama se conocen los amigos," said the man who had come in with Quartel.

"Did I ask for any of your stupid proverbs, Aforismo?" said Quartel.

"It is just a saying they have in Durango," said Aforismo. "In jail and in bed we know our friends."

He was a thin, stooped man, Aforismo, his white cotton shirt soiled with dirt and horse-droppings, his eyebrows slanting upward toward the middle of his forehead to give him a habitual expression of mournful complaint.

"Maybe you got a proverb that tells how to find out where a man pins his badge," said Quartel, looking at Crawford.

"I know one about a stitch in time—"

"Knew a Texas Ranger once who pinned it to his undershirt," said Quartel.

Bueno Bailey had looked up. "What saddle you in now?"

"It would be a good reason," said Quartel. "He had to have some reason."

"Listen," said Bueno. "That's Glenn Crawford. Sure he had some reason. A lot of reasons. But not that. He's—"

"I know who he is," said Quartel.

"Then why—"

"Innes took Tarant back to San Antonio last night," said Quartel. "Innes heard a lot of talk. There's rumor of a government marshal in the *brasada.*"

"If that's so, it's because of Crawford," said Bueno. "Kenmare couldn't get him. I wouldn't doubt they'd send a marshal after him."

"Maybe you got it inside your boot," said Quartel.

"What makes you so touchy about a badge-packer?" said Crawford.

Bailey had stood up. "Listen, Quartel, can't you get it through your thick skull, whatever Crawford is, he ain't a lawman."

"Isn't he?" Quartel studied Crawford a moment. Then he threw back his head to emit that short, harsh laugh, so loud it seemed to rock the room. It died as swiftly as it had come. His glance dropped to Crawford's legs. "So you got reasons to come back. Africano, maybe?"

"*You* haven't broken him," said Crawford.

Quartel flushed. "I will. There isn't any horse I can't break."

"He would have rolled you if you'd been a second later with that *mangana* yesterday."

"Well, I wasn't a second later," said Quartel. "Did you see that *mangana?* Nobody else could have done it so close." He thumped his barrel chest with a hairy fist. "I'm the best damn roper in the world, Crawford. I can rope better and ride farther and drink more and cuss dirtier than any *hombre* from here to Mexico City. Now let's go. I got a lot of cattle to clean out of that brush and I'm not wasting a man here to guard you."

Jacinto had come through the covered dog-run from the kitchen in time to hear Quartel. "The *señorita* will not like that," he said.

Quartel turned angrily toward him. "You in Merida's *corrida* or mine."

"Yours, Quartel, *madre de Dios,* yours," said Jacinto. "Still she won't like that. Only last night I heard her say—"

"*Punta en boca,*" said Quartel. "Shut your mouth. All right, Crawford. We got the horses saddled."

Crawford's boots made a hesitant scrape on the hard-packed adobe floor; then he took a breath, and walked toward the door. Jacinto waddled after him, sweat glistening in the wrinkles between the rolls of fat forming his face. He caught Crawford's arm, trying to stop him.

"Listen, *señor,*" he said breathlessly. "Don't let them take you out there. Merida is against it. I heard her and Huerta arguing about it. Just wait till I tell her and she'll stop Quartel. Don't let them get you out there." Quartel had moved outside to let Crawford through the door. The heat of the sun struck him like a blow on the face as he stepped out with Jacinto still tugging at him. "I'm telling you, *señor,* don't be a fool. If they get you—"

"Dammittohell!" screamed Quartel, and stepped in to spin around with his arm held out. The backhand blow caught Jacinto squarely in the face. Jacinto's hand clutched Crawford's arm spasmodically as the blow knocked him backward, jerking Crawford off balance. Then Jacinto's three hundred pounds of sweating brown flesh struck the wall of the bunkhouse. The building shuddered, and a shower of pale adobe flakes descended on the huge Mexican as he slid to the ground.

Quartel stood there a moment, his face diffused with blood till it looked positively negroid, his whole body shaking with rage. For the first time, the utter, primal violence of the man struck Crawford. Without a word, Quartel turned and walked across the compound.

The true suffocation in all this heat seemed to close in on Crawford as he moved to follow Quartel. He found himself breathing with a heavy effort. Cabezablanca was standing by the group of horses near the corral. The white-headed man held his Winchester tenderly.

"How are you, Crawford?" he said softly. Crawford glanced at him without answering, and Cabezablanca's eyes narrowed and he ran one finger up and down the gleaming barrel of his carbine. "You still refuse to be civil with me. That is unfortunate. I am a very dangerous man, Crawford."

"That's your horse." Quartel nodded at a ewe-necked old paint standing near the corral fence. It had rheumy eyes and rope scars all over its gaunt shoulders and a saddleback the shape of hickory bow and the weediest legs Crawford had ever laid eyes on. Yet, standing even this near the animal, Crawford could feel that nebulous excitation begin to rise in him. Or was it excitation? The sweat broke out on his palms. In a sudden burst of anger, he clamped his fists shut.

"What kind of crowbait is this?" he said.

Quartel shrugged. "I thought—I mean your legs—"

"I told you that was over." Crawford did not know whether the anger was at himself or at Quartel. He might not have said it under more control. "I can ride anything you can!"

"Africano?" said Quartel. He saw Crawford stiffen and grow pale, and his laugh had a scraping sound. "Never mind, Crawford, never mind. You won't have to fork the *puro negro*. He ain't broke yet. You saw that yesterday." Then the laughter left Quartel. He jerked a thumb at the paint. "Get on."

"The hell." Crawford had bent forward slightly, his whole body rigid. That bitter intensity had drawn the flesh taut across his cheeks beneath his scrubby beard. He turned abruptly toward the corral.

"Where you going?" shouted Quartel.

"To get a decent horse," said Crawford, without turning back. "You want to try and stop me?"

He was sweating again. It was a little sorrel pony with a running walk so relaxed Crawford could hear the teeth pop at every step like a Tennessee walker, and a rocking-chair would have been harder on a man. Yet he was sweating again.

"They say the *hombres* who curse the *brasada* most love it the best," said Aforismo. "You must love it like a woman."

Crawford turned his head sharply toward the man. He hadn't realized he had been swearing out loud. It hadn't been at the brush. It was so confused now, inside and out. It was hard to breathe, and the muscles across his stomach were tight as a stretched dally, and he could feel the pain spreading from his hips. *All the symptoms of genuine pain.* Was that what Huerta had said? *Sweating, trembling, tears in the eyes.* The doctor's voice was in his ears, suave, insidious. *The mind plays funny tricks sometimes.* It couldn't be. Not his mind. Not *my* mind, Huerta, not *my* mind.

"Yeah," grinned Bueno Bailey, forking a big dun on Crawford's other side. "There never was a man could cuss the brush like Crawford. I'd rather listen to him talking his way through a *mogote* of chaparral than hear music."

Crawford hardly heard him. The perspiration was sticky beneath his armpits, his shirt clung to his back with it. And now it was that other, stirring in him, so confused with the pain at first he could not define it, or would not—the same thing he had felt there at the corral, watching Africano. *And worse than the pain.* No. He wasn't afraid. *I'm not afraid, Huerta.* How could he be? *How could I be? Living with horses all my life. How could I be?*

"Take it easy," snapped Bueno. "What's the matter?"

Crawford jerked the reins against his horse, realizing he had allowed it to sidle into the dun. The sorrel shifted uncertainly the other way, thumping into Aforismo's animal. This time Crawford's reining was even more violent and it caused the sorrel to shy.

Crawford was clenching his teeth now with the effort at control. His knees were like vises against the animal's sides. Just a trot, and his knees were like vises. *Oh, damn you, Crawford. Just a trot, and you're bouncing like a satchel in a spring buggy.* He felt a desperate relief sweep him as Quartel drew up ahead of them, running a finger around the inside of the red bandanna he wore.

"God, it's like a furnace," he said.

"The drier the spring the more mesquite beans in the summer," said Aforismo.

Quartel glanced keenly at Crawford, then waved his hand at a big thicket of black chaparral starting a few yards away. "That *mogote* covers two or three miles. We been through once, but it's so thick a lot of the *cimarrónes* got away from us. Crawford is riding with Bailey and me. Whitehead, you take a line through the north flank of the *mogote*. Meet us at Rio Diablo about sundown."

Cabezablanca looked at Crawford before he wheeled his horse and trotted off into the brush, followed by Aforismo. Quartel forked a big brown animal with white hairs in its tail; they called it a *pelicano*. He reined the horse violently around, flapping his stirrups out wide. He did not have to kick the animal. As soon as the *pelicano* saw those feet fly out, it bolted into a wild gallop straight for the thicket. Crawford nudged the sorrel with a heel and followed, stiffening in the saddle as he broke into a trot. Quartel made a great ripping sound tearing through the first thin fringe of mesquite. Then they were in the dry heat of the thicket.

There was no more wily animal in the world than the *ladino* of the *brasada*. These outlaw cattle made nests for themselves in the thickest *mogotes,* lying there for days at a time when hunted, their food the very thicket that surrounded them. They ate off the prickly pear and other brush within the *mogote* until it formed a veritable room, with the walls and roof of entangled chaparral and mesquite so dense that they were invisible from without. This larger thicket the men rode through was in reality formed by many smaller thickets, with game trails and open patches throughout the thinner brush surrounding the minor *mogotes*. Quartel followed one of these game trails for some time without any apparent effort to find sign. Then, abruptly, he pulled up on his reins. The heavy *pelicano* reared to an instant's stop, head jerking up to the brutal jerk on its cruel spade bit. Quartel leaned toward the *mogote* of black chaparral and Crawford was close enough now to see the man's thick nostrils flutter.

"*Cimarrónes* in here," whispered the Mexican, finally. "Outlaws. You go around to the other side, Bueno. You'll get the first chance at whatever Crawford and I scare out from here."

Bailey pulled his dun around and cut through an opening between this smaller *mogote* and another, disappearing. Quartel wiped sweat off his face with the back of his hand. He grinned pawkily at Crawford.

"How's the sorrel?" he said.

"Good enough," said Crawford. He tried to relax. But he knew what was coming. It would be fast now. If there were *ladinos* in there, it would be fast.

"Hola!"

Quartel's hoarse shout startled the sorrel so much it almost pitched Crawford off. Grabbing wildly with his legs, Crawford saw the Mexican's stirrups flapped out that way. The *pelicano* bolted into a headlong gallop and crashed bodily into that dense mass of chaparral, ripping a great hole in the *mogote*. Crawford knew a moment's painful hesitation, fighting his spooked sorrel, then he gave the animal its head and booted it in the flanks.

The horse went through the hole Quartel had left. The brush formed but a thin wall, and the sorrel burst into the opening beyond with a startling abruptness. In these first few moments Crawford felt nothing but a blurred impression of externals. He saw Quartel's *pelicano* ahead, trailing white brush from its scarred hide and dripping mesquite berries in its wake. He had a vivid picture of three gaunt cattle leaping to their feet beyond, and knew a faint, transitory surprise that he should notice such an insignificant detail as the hair rubbed off the knees of the white heifer, showing that she had been crawling the brush instead of walking, in order to remain hidden from the recent roundup. Then the trio of *cimarrónes* had wheeled away from Quartel's horse and crashed through the opposite wall. The deafening sound and the swift, blinding movement stunned Crawford's senses as he went through after Quartel.

"*Bueno!*" screamed Bailey, appearing from somewhere beyond with his dally rope spinning in a California throw, coming up from underneath so it would not catch on the overhanging brush, "*bueno,*" the loop snaking about the forefeet of the lead steer. The ground shook as the steer went down and Bailey's horse was stiff-legging to a stop, Bailey swinging down to run for the kicking steer with a peal. He had done the whole thing with such incredible speed that before Crawford had passed, Bailey had the steer's hind legs hog-tied with the short rawhide peal and was dragging him to a coma tree, where he would leave him hitched until they were ready to take him back to the spread. Then Bailey was behind, and Quartel and Crawford were smashing through a thin stretch of mesquite after the other two.

No riding in the world could compare with popping the brush. A *brasadero* might easily take a job on a spread outside the brush and make good, but a hand used to the prairies seldom succeeded in becoming a brush hand. It took consummate skill to ride at a dead run through the brush after cattle like this. And Quartel had that skill. Ahead of Crawford, he made a bobbing swaying figure on that big *pelicano,* rarely holding his seat on top of the saddle, incessantly swinging off to the side or ducking down forward or jerking back and forth. The two *ladinos* raced beneath a post oak branch so low it scraped hide off their backs, and Crawford expected to see Quartel rein violently around it. But the Mexican merely swung one leg off and hung down the side of his horse like an Indian, his thick right arm hooked over the *pelicano's* neck. The oak branch knocked Quartel's sombrero off his head—he would have lost it but for the tie-thong—and tore at the cantle of the saddle so violently the whole rigging shrieked. There was a great mass of thorny junco just beyond the tree, growing as high as the *pelicano's* head, and a less skillful man would have been ripped to bloody shreds before he got back onto the saddle. Crawford could hear Quartel's violent grunt and thought sure the man was swinging up too soon and would be knocked back down by that branch. But Quartel had gauged it to a nicety. His spasmodic lurch upward took him back into the saddle just in time. The junco merely scraped his left leg as he thundered by.

"Hola," he shouted wildly, "hola, you crazy *cimarrónes*, I'm right on your tail, hola!"

Something within Crawford rebelled as he neared that spot Quartel had passed through. He felt his hands tugging on the reins, and the sorrel lost all its collection, thrown off balance as it tried to pull out of its mad gallop into a trot. Crawford was panting in a heavy, frustrated way as he shifted through the spot beneath the post oak branch and past the junco bush. And now it was strong enough in him to have a palpable grip, like a great hand squeezing his vitals. The first action had been violent enough to carry him along with it, but now that was over, and slowing like that had been the final error.

The muscles across his stomach were knotting with nervous tension, and his legs quivered against the side of the sorrel. He leaned forward, and the horse gathered itself to break into a gallop ahead. But somehow he could not move his feet against the animal's side. Somehow his hands would not relax their hold on the reins.

"What's the matter, Crawford?"

It was Bueno Bailey, tearing in from behind, and Crawford realized he had been sobbing to himself, huddled over his horse that way. "Nothing, damn you, nothing," he shouted and booted the sorrel so hard it whinnied in surprise and pain, rearing up and then bolting headlong after Quartel. Crawford had one more glimpse of the Mexican before he disappeared from sight, chousing after those two animals. A malignant branch of chaparral reached out for Quartel's head, and he dodged that and then swayed back the other way in time to miss being blinded by a clump of mesquite berries. Then he reined his horse around a growth of prickly pear and swung down off the flank as the animal burst through a last dense growth of chaparral with branches so low the *ladinos* had found trouble going through, and then he was out of sight.

Keep your eyes open, keep your eyes open. It kept spinning through Crawford's head like that, the fundamental dictum of brush-popping. If a man closed his eyes once he was lost. Crawford had seen more than one hand knocked from his horse because a branch appearing suddenly out of nowhere had caused him to shut his eyes and dodge blindly.

The sorrel was going at a frenzied, headlong pace now, caught up in the wild excitement of the chase, with the drumming pound of Bueno Bailey's dun off to the flank and the deafening crash of mesquite and chaparral echoing about them. All he could do was dodge and duck. He found himself gripping the horn with one white-knuckled hand. Cursing bitterly, he tore it off, jerking violently aside just in time to miss being raked by a thick mat of mesquite. And all the time it was going through him, *keep your eyes open,* and he couldn't.

A branch of *chaparro prieto* loomed before his face and he jerked aside and blackness blotted out sight. He heard someone yelling and did not know it was himself till he had opened his eyes again. It could not have been from pain because he had missed the chaparro. But the instant he opened his eyes, leaning off to one side that way, junco and retama were clawing at his face. With his eyes open he would have been able to see them in time to dodge. As it was, the myriad claws of the allthorn raked his flesh like the stroke of a jaguar's paw. Again his eyes clamped shut, and he tore himself out of the tangle. If it had been a post oak it would have knocked him off.

He did not know whether the screams were inside his head now or whether he actually voiced them. He felt his hands jerking desperately on the reins, but the sorrel was running wild, and he had lost control of the horse as well as himself. He was swept with violent, spasmodic waves of virulent anger at himself and pain that grew more knifing each time it struck from his loins and fear that turned his mind to a kaleidoscope of uncontrolled sensations. He was clinging with both hands to the horn now, his eyes closed, sobbing and screaming. The sorrel sideswiped a post oak. A low branch knocked Crawford backward with the blow. He reeled back to an upright position, swimming in a stunned agony. Somewhere, dimly, in what was left of his consciousness he realized there was only one thing to do. If he tried to keep on the horse any longer this way he would be battered into pulp. Yet, knowing it, there was no will left in him to act. Even that swift thought of it caused a new spasm of awful fear.

Reeling, swaying, his eyes clamped shut, his ducking jacket ripped and torn, he rode on madly through the thicket. He crashed through a mesquite thicket, and the brush clawed his cheeks to shreds. Chaparral beat him aside time and time again. His screams were hoarse and incoherent now, hardly human. The lathered, frothing wild-eyed horse was in a frenzy, its hoofs drumming the ground in a dim tattoo beneath the deafening, incessant crash of brush. Then that last blow caught him, square across the belly. It must have been a low branch. His desperate grip was torn from the saddle horn, and he was swept over the cantle and off the sorrel's rump, doubled over. He had one lucid thought before his head struck the ground, blotting out all thought.

Huerta was right!

Chapter Four

Unreasoning Fear

DUSK HELD ITS OWN singular aspect. There was something hushed about the brush at this time. Not the dead oppressive silence of noon. There were many small sounds, but the bizarre, velvety clutch of twilight seemed to subdue them. A hooty owl called tentatively from a hackberry down in some yonder draw. An invisible jack rabbit made a dim, staccato thump hopping through a distant clearing, then halted. Nearer by a lizard rustled sibilantly through the foot-deep layer of decaying brush, which for eons had been dropping from the bushes to pile up on the ground.

It was these sounds, one by one, which impinged on Glenn Crawford's consciousness. Then the fetid odor of the mold beneath him. His face felt stiff and painful. It caused him a great effort to reach up to his cheek. The rips and tears made great gaps in his beard and his whole face was covered with dried blood. Finally he sat up, shaking his head dully. Three hours? Four hours? What time had it been? It was hard to think. He shook his head again. Early afternoon anyway. And this was—

That brought him up straight. They hadn't found him? It was strange. It was wrong, somehow. They hadn't found him. Wrong. They were better trackers than that. All of them. If Quartel could ride like that he could track like that.

He got up with great difficulty and fell down again. His head was spinning. When he got to his knees once more, the shreds of his ducking jacket bound his arms, and when he fell that second time, he went full on his face, unable to get his hands in front of him. In a fit of anger he tore the remains of the jacket off. The third time he managed to remain upright. As he stood there, the first thought of the horse came to him. He felt that pain begin in his loins. Just the thought of it!

With a sobbing curse he broke into a stumbling run at the first thicket of brush. He halted himself before he had reached the *mogote*. He was breathing heavily and his lips were pinched. He held out his hand before him. It shook visibly. He closed his eyes a moment, face twisted. Then he took a deep breath and opened them again, staring about the clearing. There was a great torn place in one thicket on the other side. He moved over there at a deliberate walk. The hole in the brush was big enough to walk through; beyond that was another open patch and then a second small thicket torn asunder by the passage of a heavy body. It was full night by the time he found the sorrel that way, following the trail it had made bursting through the brush. The animal stood in a clearing, head hanging wearily, dried lather forming dirty yellow patterns on its freshly scarred hide.

Crawford was about to step into the open when he caught himself. There was a dim rustling in the brush to his left. His face turned that way sharply. The noise ceased after a moment. He shook his head and went out to get the horse.

"Stand still, you crazy fool," he said, "stand still now, I'm not going to hurt you, just stand still, that's it, hold it."

The animal had started to shift away, but his soothing voice quieted it. He moved in close and ran his hand reassuringly along its rump and down its side. Then, as he stood with his face toward it that way, close enough so that the heat of its body reached his belly, it began to come again. That insidious, stirring, prickling sensation deep in his loins. That hollow sickness growing in his stomach till it approached nausea; the sweat breaking out on his face and beneath his armpits.

The curse had a strangled sound in his throat, as he bent to get the trailing reins. He wouldn't walk back to the spread. No matter what else, he wouldn't give them that satisfaction. He stopped, with his hand not yet touching the end of the reins. Even in the dark, bending over like that, he could see the footprints. The sorrel's hoofs had made their dim impression all over the decaying vegetation covering the gound. But here and there, where the horse had not blotted it out, was a smaller, deeper imprint, like that of a boot heel. He remained stooped over it for a moment that way. Then, slowly, he started to lift the reins. They were caught on something. He reached down and found the ends tied about a long stake of wood embedded deeply beneath the rotting brush.

Crawford slipped the reins off the stick and rose beside the horse. Slowly he put his weight against its neck. His breath had a small, swift sound. The horse gradually shifted around under that pressure until it stood broadside between Crawford and the direction that small rustling had come from when he first entered the thicket.

"Now." He spoke to the horse softly, sliding his hands up the reins till they were directly beneath the bit, and pulling gently forward. "Let's go. Let's go. Take it easy. Let's go."

The animal moved toward the fringe of brush surrounding the clearing. Crawford walked close in by its side, tugging incessantly forward on the reins, talking in that soft low tone. The animal's hoofs crackled in the brush underfoot. It snorted once, pulling peevishly at his tight grip on the shanks of the bit. He twisted them upward slightly and the horse responded to the bit against its roof, quieting. They had almost reached the edge of the *mogote* when the shot crashed.

The horse was jerked over against Crawford by the

force of the bullet going through its body. Then it reared into the air, screaming. Desperately Crawford tried to retain his hold on the reins, yanking the horse on ahead, throwing the whole weight of his body into it. He managed to fight the plunging, rearing animal a couple more steps toward the brush. Then the beast's violent spasms tore his grip loose of the reins. With the animal still forming a shield in that last instant, he threw himself in a headlong dive for the thicket. Another shot roared behind him, and the horse screamed again, and then Crawford was rolling into the crackling, tearing mesquite thicket. He came to his feet, pawing a cluster of berries out of his face, and plunged blindly on into the *mogote.*

For a long, blind run, the only sound was that incessant deafening crash of brush all about him. He burst through that first thicket and crossed a game trail and clattered into another *mogote.* Black chaparral this time, and stabbing junco and maddening prickly pear. Then an open patch. And another *ramadero.* White brush and golden huisache that filled the air with a vague, viscid odor of honey. Then that was gone and the spines of the agarita tore at his face. He broke through the agarita into a game trail that wound its secretive way through the *mogotes,* and he stumbled down that till it petered out into more mesquite. Halfway through, the spread of mesquite became entwined with chaparro *prieto* and Spanish dagger that met his every movement with a vicious stab of its dirklike growth. He found himself fighting a frantic, useless battle to penetrate this thicket farther; it had brought him to a complete stop and, standing there, chest heaving, face dripping sweat, he could see that the impenetrable *mogote* was on the rim of a draw, and that it grew on down into the bottom of the draw, choking it full. Even if he could manage to fight his way through the thicket, he would be exposed, crossing that draw. The realization came to him in a dim, spasmodic way, with no true reasoning behind it, for he was still filled with that animal panic.

He whirled back and fought his way out of the mesquite. And then, crossing the comparatively open space of the game trail, it came to him. He stopped there. Tears squeezed from his eyes with the effort it caused him to control his breath so he could hear more clearly. It came again, small, distant, yet distinct enough. The faint rattle of mesquite berries, brushed by a passing body. The soft snap of decaying vegetation beneath a careless foot. Again it was no reasoning process. Just a wave of instinctive, animal realization of how he was trapped. Face twisting with frustrated rage, Crawford backed slowly, almost involuntarily, across the game trail into the mesquite thicket again. He moved as far back as he could, upright, and then he got down on his belly and crawled in until the roots and trunks and foliage became too thick even for that, and then he stopped.

His shirt was drenched with sweat and the perspiration dripped into his eyes, blinding and stinging. Gnats began to float in, attracted by the sweat and the blood of his scratches. At first he fought them. He rubbed his palms viciously against his face, mashing the maddening insects. He slapped wildly, gasping virulent curses. It only seemed to draw more. With a myriad of the gnats mashed wetly against the cut, bleeding, stinging, itching flesh of his face, and with a veritable cloud of them buzzing about his upper body, he put his head at last into his arms, and a bitter, hoarse sobbing arose mutedly from him.

At last he stopped even that. He lay there in utter, hopeless defeat. His crashing passage through the brush had frightened all the small animals into silence, but now the sounds of them began again. A hooty owl started to call, somewhere far out in the brush. Then, a coyote

mourning in some distant draw. The singing of a mock-
ingbird that had stayed awake to welcome the rising
moon. The rustle of lizards through the decay. And
that other sound. That desultory, intermittent sound of
someone moving out there.

A thin scream rang out with terrifying abruptness,
jerking Crawford's head up. He lay that way a moment,
up on his hands, rigid, trembling with strain. Then he
lowered himself again. Only an ocelot, somewhere, out
there, a big cat down from the mountains across the Rio
maybe. And now, lying there, with the first awful sense of
defeat losing its edge, the other began to come. They
thought they had him? Damn them. Whoever it was,
damn them. The anger grew in him till it struggled with
the defeat. It thickened the blood in his throat till he
almost choked. Had him trapped? The hell. Kill him
like that? Without a gun, without anything. Think he'd
just wait? *Try it. Come on, try it. I'm here. Try it.*

It was going through his head while he squirmed
about beneath the low overhanging branches of chaparral, scratching his face and hands anew on barbed nopal
and the harsh mesquite. Finally he found a maguey
plant, close to the trail. He had no knife, and he had to
tear at it with his fingers. They were ripped and bleeding by the time he had torn the first strip of the leathery
plant.

The Mexicans cured the strips in brine and in the sun
to supple it for their ropes. Crawford could do nothing
but braid the stiff lengths together. And all the time,
out there, approaching with the deliberateness of a man
knowing the confidence of complete advantage, those
sounds, rising with deadly intermittence over the other
sounds. The soft crunch of a boot heel driving through
the layer of rotting vegetation that covered the ground.
The sibilant harshness of mesquite scraping leather.
Crawford worked with swift desperation till he had a line

long enough; then he knotted a hondo into one end and formed a loop. It took him half a dozen throws across the game trail to snag one of the low chaparral branches in a *mogote* over there. Then he hooked the line beneath a root on the opposite side of the trail so that it crossed the trail itself on the ground. He moved back into his own thicket as far as the line would permit. Then it was the waiting. Working with the rope that way, there had been no time to think. But now it had begun to come.

En la cárcel y en la cama se conocen los amigos.

Crawford felt his whole body grow rigid with a palpable jerk. He almost turned his head to see who had spoken. A muffled sound escaped him as he realized it had only been in his mind. The *brasada* could do that to a man, this way. In bed and in jail we know our friends? Sure. Maybe it was Aforismo. What did it matter.

The hooty owl stopped for a while, and there were only small rustlings in the underbrush. Then the sound again, returning. A sibilant, crushed, snapping sound.

I am a very dangerous man, Crawford.

This time he did not stiffen. It jumped through his brain so vividly he could have sworn it was spoken. Yet he did not stiffen. All right. So maybe it was Whitehead. All right.

Moonlight spilled through his thicket suddenly, and he realized how long he had lain there. The rising moon made skeletal monsters of the chaparral bushes across the yellow river of the game trail, only adding to the haunted tension filling Crawford. Thoughts moved uncontrollably through his head now.

Please, no violence. I was born for laughter and wassail and song—

No. Not Jacinto. Anybody else. Even Wallace Tarant. But not big, fat, grumbling Hyacinth of the River. The gnats had found Crawford again. He dared not move as they buzzed fitfully about his face, stinging, maddening.

He closed his eyes, gritting his teeth. Then he opened them again. That would not do.

He thought he would go crazy. His hands twitched with the impulse to slap at them. His body cried out for movement to escape their insane buzzing. Each sting made him jerk spasmodically.

Bueno—

Sure, Bailey. Sure. Crawford could imagine Bailey doing that sort of thing. All right, Bailey. Come on, Bailey. Let's get it over with, Bailey.

He tried to stop thinking like that. There were so many possibilities. He tried to stop considering them. A man could go loco that way. He could go loco and jump right up out of the thicket and run screaming down the game trail right into the arms of that bushwhacker, whoever it was. A man could go loco anyway. The ocelot screamed out there again, filling the night with a thin feral madness. It was all madness. The gnats and the screaming cat and the howling coyote and the crackling mesquite and the thoughts Crawford couldn't stop whirling faster and faster through his head till he wanted to beat it against the ground.

You'll excuse me. An old complaint.

Huerta? Sure, why not? It could be him. It could be any of them.

I knew a Ranger once that pinned it to his undershirt.

Yeah. Even Quartel. The ocelot or Quartel or the hooty owl or any of them.

He lay there, wanting to cry, his fists clenched around the rope till they hurt, his eyes squeezed tight with the terrible effort he made to control himself. Finally he opened them again, staring down the trail. It would be getting him, too, out there. If it was getting Crawford it would get the other man just as much. The *brasada.* That's what it was. The *brasada.* Enough to drive any man loco like this. And it would be getting him, too, out there.

The ocelot screamed. Crawford's lips pulled off his teeth in a wolfish grin. That get you, Bailey? That get you, Whitehead? Like it got me? The hooty owl began to talk. Crawford's grin spread. That get you? Huerta? Sort of scary, isn't it? Jacinto? Stop maybe, and look around. Sweat maybe. Like me. Aforismo? Sure. Sure it got them. They were as nervous as hell. Whoever it was, he was as nervous as hell. Crawford wanted to laugh suddenly. He was bathed suddenly in a cold sweat. Then heat flooded up from his loins. It was like a fever.

Or was it the waiting? Or the *brasada*. Sure, the *brasada*. He'd felt this way before out in it. At night. Not so much, maybe. But then he hadn't been waiting for a man with a gun to come and kill him either.

The decay was damp from his sweat beneath his belly and legs. His eyes ached from peering into the brush all about him. The gnats kept clouding his vision. But now the man was closer. Each minute sibilance crashed through Crawford's head like thunder. He could tell when the man's clothing brushed a clump of mesquite berries and knocked some to the ground. There was a peculiar rattling quality to that. He could tell when the man stepped on a prickly pear. It had a squashing sound. And when he shoved aside some chaparral. That held a hollow thump. And pulled aside some huisache. Sighing, like the wind.

I'm a very dangerous man, Crawford. Sure. Sure you are, Whitehead. Come on. I'll show you who's dangerous. I knew a man once who pinned it to his undershirt. All right. One more time, Quartel. One more time around and I'll show you who's dangerous. Made for laughter and wassail and song? Come on. I'm waiting. An old complaint? You'll have a complaint, Huerta. In bed and in jail—

Then it was the shadowy figure moving out of the

darkness down the trail, and Crawford yanked on the maguey and it slipped off the branch and the branch snapped up with a soft crackle and caused the figure to whirl that way, his gun crashing, his back toward the thicket in which Crawford lay.

"Maybe you're a dangerous man," screamed Crawford in a terrible release, leaping to his feet and throwing himself bodily at the man, who was still firing wildly into the opposite thicket, "but this is one bronc you'll wish to hell you never climbed on!"

Chapter Five

Huerta Makes a Proposition

At dawn, it was the birds, mostly, during the spring months, like this. They filled the dim undulations of brush with a constant, shrill twittering. Bobwhites shrieked from a draw full of white brush, and blue quail cooed beneath the *cejas* of green brazil, and turkeys gobbled down in a dry creek bed where they were fattening on elm mast.

Through all this treble cacophony, Glenn Crawford walked heavily up the road leading the shaggy black cow pony. It was Jacinto who saw him first. Though the sun had not yet risen, smoke curled from the kitchen, and the gross Mexican was just outside the door filling the coffeepot from the water butt. It cost him some effort to straighten up when he caught sight of Crawford. He stared blankly. Then he dropped the big coffeepot with a clang and began running his way, grunting as each foot struck the ground, his short, bandy legs looking as if they would collapse every time the prodigious weight of his torso descended on them in a step.

"*Dios,* Crawford," he shouted. "*Válgame Dios.* What happened? *Que hace?* Who is it? Are you all right? What happened?"

He was halfway to Crawford by the time Aforismo stumbled into view at the bunkhouse door, pulling bare brown legs into his stiff, greasy *chivarras* and blinking sleepily. Someone must have asked him what it was, for he grunted something over his shoulder and came on out. Jacinto had reached Crawford by the time he got to the front of the house, and it was there Crawford halted the horse. The tremendous Mexican stood with his great belly heaving from the run, staring blankly at White-head. He started to reach out and touch the man, then dropped his hand.

"Is—is he—"

"Yes," said Crawford, watching Aforismo come from the bunkhouse and Quartel step out the door now, yawning and cursing. The shutter on an upstairs window clattered against the dilapidated weatherboarding, and Huerta leaned out to look down a moment. Then he withdrew his head, and Crawford could hear movement from within his room. Quartel came across the compound after Aforismo, slipping a dirty cotton shirt over his head.

"What happened?" he said. He looked at the body slung across the horse without much expression in his face. What lay in his eyes was not apparent till he got closer. They were narrowed, and the pupils held a strange oblong felinity.

"*Es muerto,*" said Jacinto stupidly.

"I know he's dead," said Quartel. "What happened?"

"Out in the brush," said Crawford, watching Quartel.

The Mexican looked at him, then glanced at the horse. He reached out to pull the Winchester from beneath the stirrup leather, opening the front end of the magazine and tilting the gun down. Two copper rim-fires clinked into his calloused palm.

"Looks like he did a lot of shooting," said Quartel.

"He always carried that gun in one hand when he rode," said Jacinto. "I told him he'd fall and break his neck sometime."

"Did you?" said Quartel. He was studying Crawford, shaking the two .44 shells up and down in his closed hand. "You still haven't told us what happened."

"His neck's broken," said Jacinto hopefully.

Quartel allowed his narrowed eyes to observe the odd way Cabezablanca's head hung, twisted around from the line of his shoulders. "That's what it looks like. Where did you find him?"

"Yes," said Doctor Huerta, from the door. "Where did you find him, Crawford?"

He had on a gaudy black-and-gold dressing-gown with satin lapels and slippers of red leather. His face had never looked more dissolute. The dim light seemed to draw out the singular, jaundiced corruption of his sallow flesh. His heavy lids were almost closed over his eyes, veined and pouched, and one of them twitched visibly. He had both hands in the pockets of his bathrobe, and they were visibly closed into fists. Merida stood behind him. She had on a house gown of blue cashmere, evidently donned hurriedly. There was something Indian about her dark, aquiline face; her black hair hanging long and straight about her shoulders.

"I told you," said Crawford. "Out in the brush."

"You didn't tell me," said Huerta.

"I told Quartel," said Crawford.

"He didn't tell me what happened," said Quartel.

"To Crawford," said Merida, "or Whitehead?"

"Yes," said Doctor Huerta, moving tiredly across the porch. "What did happen to you, Crawford?"

"We ain't interested in that now," said Quartel. "I'd like to know what happened to Whitehead first."

"You seemed interested yesterday," said Merida. "You were quite upset that you had lost Crawford in the brush."

"What have you got in your hand?" said Huerta.

"A gun," Quartel told him.

"Don't be obtuse," said Huerta. "I mean the other hand."

Quartel opened his fingers. The two shells glinted dully in the growing light. Somewhere out back of the bunkhouse a rooster crowed. Both Huerta and Merida looked for a long moment at the two cartridges. Slowly,

Huerta's jaded eyes moved to Crawford, and the heavy, blue lids were lifted farther open.

"You say his neck is broken?" Huerta asked nobody in particular.

"Jacinto said his neck was broken," said Quartel.

"Well," said the woman impatiently, "is it?"

Huerta drew a weary breath and came slowly down the sagging steps and around the horse. "Yes," he nodded, without taking his hands from his pockets. "Broken."

"Like in a fall?" That pathetic hope was in Jacinto's voice again.

Huerta took one of his hands out. His long, pale fingers moved slightly across Cabezablanca's head and face, sifting the dense white hair and testing the skull with a professional casualness. "No contusions about the head or face."

Huerta was running his forefinger delicately across the back of Cabezablanca's shirt now, flattening it over the resilient planes of the man's back. Then he moved around to the other side of the shaggy horse, tugging at the man's pants legs. "No other wounds either," he said at last. His head turned slowly till he was looking at Crawford. Something had begun to dissipate the jaded glaze from those eyes, something that grew in them as he watched Crawford. He spoke, however, to Quartel. "How many shots does that Winchester hold?"

"It's an 1866 with King's improvements," said Quartel. "Thirteen."

"Oh." It was a soft, hissing intonation. Then Huerta motioned toward the bunkhouse with the hand he had out. "Better take him down and bury him out back of the bunkhouse."

Quartel jerked the Winchester at Crawford. "Let's go."

"No," said Huerta, putting that hand back in his pocket and walking up the steps to the porch. "I think Crawford had better stay here at the house for breakfast. You did such a poor job of keeping tabs on him yesterday."

Quartel's face darkened and he took a quick breath before he spoke the word. "Huerta—"

"Yes?" said Huerta, turning around at the top of the steps to face Quartel. He leaned forward slightly, his satanic brows arched upward, those heavy lids slipping down across his eyes. There was a faint, inquiring smile on his thin, bloodless lips. For a moment Quartel stood there staring at him, mouth still open a little. The rooster crowed again. A chachalaca started scolding his mate out in the thicket. With an abrupt jerk, Quartel turned to catch up the trailing reins of the pony and started off toward the bunkhouse in that stiff-legged walk of his, wooden boot heels thumping in a swift, hard tattoo against the ground. Aforismo watched him go a moment, scratching his bare stomach absently.

"You can't tell a man's been picking tunas just because he has nopal thorns all over his coat," he said.

Crawford's boots made a soft muffled sound across the Aubusson rug of the living-room. He lowered himself heavily into the Turkish toweling which upholstered the movable cushions of the willow chairs by the front windows. For the first time he felt fully the toll the preceding night had exacted from him. His black beard failed to hide the gaunt, driven hollows beneath his cheeks, and there was something feverish in the glow of his eyes. He stared absently about the spacious, cool room. Rockland had refurnished this chamber not two years ago, and as many times as Crawford had been in it, he could never get used to such luxury in this harsh, barren land. Huerta had followed him into the house, halting in the entrance hall for a word with Merida, and now the doctor stepped into the living-room, closing the door behind him. He stood there a moment, studying

Crawford.

"Merida will dress and be down for breakfast," he said, absently. He moved to the pier table of rich, figured British oak at one side of the room, opening one of the doors to lift out a cut-glass decanter. "Perhaps you would like a drink—after what happened, no?" His face managed to convey the effort the slightest physical exertion seemed to cause him, as he poured the liquor. Then his red Chinese slippers slid over the Aubusson's thick nap to Crawford. As he bent forward to hand Crawford the drink, their glances met. Perhaps it was a trick of the illumination from the window. The pupils of Huerta's eyes seemed to dilate and contract and dilate again, small pin points of glittering light flaring and dying and flaring once more beneath the jet-black surface. It filled Crawford with a vague dizziness. "Why did you bring Whitehead back, Crawford?" murmured the doctor. "It seems to me you were rather in a position to escape, out there." He waited a moment, but Crawford did not answer. "When you first came, I considered it necessary to guard you," said Huerta, finally. "Perhaps I was taking undue precautions. It seems you would have stayed anyway. Why, Crawford? Do you still maintain you didn't murder Rockland?"

"That's right." It came from Crawford in a flat defiance.

"Then the only way you could prove your innocence would be to find who really did murder Rockland," said Huerta. "Do you think the murderer is here?"

"I have no doubt of it," said Crawford.

"Just what did happen out there?" Huerta said softly, bending toward Crawford with the liquor.

Crawford took the drink, downed it neat before answering. "What do you think?"

"I think you surprised a lot of people," said Huerta. "And gave them a different estimation of you than they had possessed before." He leaned backward slightly. "Why should Whitehead want to kill you?"

"Who said he did?"

"I never knew such a secretive man," said Huerta. "You refuse to give one inch, don't you? Very well. Let us assume that Whitehead wanted to kill you. Why should he?"

"Whitehead was Quartel's man?" said Crawford.

"Quartel is the foreman here," Huerta's agile mind had connected that even while he spoke, and his head tilted forward in a faint acquiescence. "All right. Why should Quartel want you killed?"

"He seemed to think I was a lawman," Crawford muttered.

"Is that sufficient reason?"

"You haven't been in the *brasada* long, have you?" said Crawford. "It's a good form of suicide for a lawman to show up in here."

Huerta nodded that way again, studying Crawford. "It is interesting," he murmured, "to watch it."

That took Crawford off guard. "What?"

"The way it works in you," said Huerta. "You're conscious of it all the time, Crawford, whether in the proximity of horses or not."

"I don't know what you're talking about," said Crawford, getting up from the chair with such violence that he pulled one of the rich blue pillows off with him. He paced across the room in swift, inhibited strides. Huerta watched him a moment, putting the jade holder languidly to his lips. He did not smile, but the heavy blue lids, narrowing across his eyes with a feline torpidity, managed to convey a certain condescending amusement. His pale, pinched nostrils fluttered, emitting twin streamers of smoke.

"Did it ever occur to you," he said, "that the legs might not really be completely healed?"

Crawford turned to look at him a moment. "Sure," he said, finally. "Sure it occurred to me. I went to more than one doctor. They all said I was okay."

"It's not like an ordinary fracture, you realize," said Huerta. "Not like you'd take a stick and snap it, or a leg. Mashed. Not a clean severance. Crushed, Crawford, like you'd take a handful of meal and grind it beneath—"

"All right. Mashed. Crushed. All right."

Huerta allowed him to finish, then inclined his head apologetically. "It does things to the nerves. Physically, I mean. They get crushed too. Displaced. Pinched. All manner of derangement. Your bones may knit—the flesh, the skin. But the nerves. That's different. It would, ah, take a man skilled in that type of work, now, a man with experience in such things—"

"You've had a vast experience, I suppose."

Huerta shrugged. "Why don't you let me look at them. Maybe we do you an injustice. Perhaps you have sound reason for feeling the pain."

Crawford studied the man's dissolute face, trying to read what lay in the ironic twist of the lips, the narrow occultation of the eyes, wondering if this was just another variation in the game. Yet, the possibility of sincerity—

"Shall we go into the kitchen?" said Huerta. "The parlor is not exactly the place for such an examination."

Crawford knew a hesitation. Then, with a decisive abruptness he turned out into the entrance way and down the hall past the stairs. The fireplace was of stone rather than the adobe found in the Mexican dwellings; it ran almost the length of one wall. Jacinto had left a pot of soup simmering over one of the smaller pot fires to one side of the main spit. There was a plain Gothic dining-set, and Huerta pulled one of the butternut chairs from beneath the bare table, indicating that Crawford should remove his pants. That wary inhibition was in

Crawford's movements.

"You might sit on the table," said Huerta. When Crawford was seated, the doctor moved closer and bent slightly, reaching out one pale hand. It was like a woman's hand, satiny, boneless. "Can't you relax, Crawford? What's the matter? Feel any pain?"

Crawford stared in a strange fascination at the slender, spatulated fingers spidering his hairy calves. "No. No pain."

"Then why so stiff?" Huerta pressed a spot just below his knee. The strength of his grip was surprising. Then, still holding the kneecap between thumb and forefinger, he looked up. It was the same thing, again, those eyes. The pupils took on an oblique felinity, and the odd little lights flaring beneath the surface. And he began to talk, in that soft, bored, insinuating tone. "Nerve ends, you understand. Pressures. As I said, deranged. Nucleus. So on. Hm? Pain?"

"No—no—"

Perhaps it was the gusty vehemence in Crawford's voice which caused Huerta to look up. For a moment their glances met. Huerta's pupils seemed to dilate slightly. *Sure,* thought Crawford, *go ahead, make it good,* and he tried to feel the sarcasm, but somehow he couldn't, because the effect of those eyes was real, distinct, eerie.

"No pain?"

"No. No pain. No!"

Those eyes again. Contracting. Little lights flaring and dying. Just for an instant. The probing fingers. That sibilant, insistent voice.

"Here, perhaps? The flesh looks rather badly healed. Feel that? Pain?"

"No!"

"Take it easy, Crawford. I'm trying to help. Here?"

"No. I told you. I don't feel pain, damn it, I told

you—"

"Here then. Pain?"

"No—"

"Here?"

"No, damn you, no, I—"

"Pain?" Huerta's head raised abruptly. "What's the matter, Crawford?"

Crawford stood where he had stepped off the table, pulling on his faded old levis with swift, tense jerks. "Nothing. Forget it."

Huerta leaned back against the table, studying Crawford through the twin streamers of smoke he emitted. "Why does it disturb you so much, Crawford, if you feel no pain?" he asked softly.

Crawford stood there facing him, breathing heavily. "What are you trying to do, Huerta?"

"Give you, shall we say, an illustration," said Huerta. "Don't you think I know what is the matter with you, Crawford? Ever since I first saw you watching Africano out in the corral. Perhaps the others are still groping. They sense something not quite right in you, Crawford. But they don't know for sure, yet. I know, Crawford." He said the last softly, positively, watching Crawford. He took a drag on the cigarette. "It must be a terrible thing to live with constantly. It makes two personalities out of you, really, Crawford. In these flashes of bitter defiance, I see what you must have been before. The strength. The courage. But the other is always there, isn't it, working beneath, stirring in you, weakening you, tearing at you. The pain that comes whenever you get near a horse. And the fear, Crawford. And more and more, not just when you're near a horse. All the time. That lack of confidence, that constant indecision. It won't lessen. It will grow, Crawford, until you are that way completely, until these flashes of your former self cease to come. I told you about that miner in Monterrey—"

"You told me!" Crawford choked off the shout, staring sullenly at Huerta. He spoke finally, again, controlling it with hoarse effort. "Think I don't know."

"You *do* know," said Huerta. "However, it is not hopeless. For most diseases, there is a cure, even for those of the mind. Doctors are only human beings. They can only cure what they have the knowledge to cure. If the men you went to were not experienced in this type of thing, it does not mean there is no hope."

"Are you suggesting—that you—"

"Why not?" shrugged Huerta. "I've had experience in such cases. Is it inconceivable to you?"

"Why?" said Crawford.

Huerta studied his cigarette. "I don't quite understand."

"I mean why should you do it," said Crawford.

"I am no altruist," said Huerta. "A doctor usually gets paid."

"You know I haven't got any money," Crawford said. Huerta did not answer, leaning against the table and studying Crawford through narrowed eyes. "You're offering me some kind of proposition?" Crawford asked him.

"You might call it that," said Huerta. "As I said before, we think your quarrel with Rockland was over more than the way he acquired Delcazar's land."

"Was it?"

"You know what I mean," said Huerta.

"Maybe I haven't got what you want."

"I think you have," said Huerta.

"Have you got a license?" said Crawford.

It was the first time he had ever seen Huerta taken off guard. There was no change of expression in the doctor's face. Just that moment's hesitation. It was enough to give Crawford a certain satisfaction.

"License?"

"M.D.," said Crawford. "Every doctor I've seen had it pinned on his wall. Two or three, some of them. How about yours?"

Huerta drew a heavy breath. "I won't dignify that with an answer."

"I didn't think so," said Crawford. "That's one reason I won't take your proposition. I don't think you could cure me of the stomach-ache. I don't think you're a doctor. I don't think you ever were."

"My dear fellow, I spent fourteen years in the Mexican army—"

"So did a lot of butchers. If you operated on anybody, I'll bet a pink cow to a blind hoot owl it was with a machete right up in the ranks."

"Crawford, my medical reputation has never been ques—" It had come out of Huerta involuntarily, and he stopped himself with a distinct effort. He stood there a moment, the anger flushing his sallow face dully as he must have realized how far he had let himself go. Deliberately, he allowed himself to settle back against the table. He closed his eyes when he took a drag on the cigarette, did not open them as he exhaled, and spoke. "Let us consider the negative side of my proposition, then. Your condition can be used against you, Crawford. You could be driven quite mad. Not obvious crudities. Not the type of thing Quartel would use. Not making you ride a horse or letting you watch Africano. Not anything as simple to get away from. Merely suggestion, Crawford. Your mind will do the rest. Little things. Insidious things.

"Like the story of a miner who got crushed in a cave-in down at Monterrey. Did that stay with you a long time, Crawford? At night, perhaps, you'd wake up. Remembering. Wondering. Innuendoes, Crawford. Insinuations. Things for the mind to retain and savor. Because it *is* your mind. I showed you that with the examination. It isn't your legs. That doesn't give you the fear. It's what a man could work with, Crawford, a doctor, who knew every stimulus, every reaction." He took the butt of his cigarette from the jade holder, tossing it absently into the fireplace. Then, still watching the holder, he spoke again, sibilantly. "Do you doubt my ability to do it, Crawford, if necessary?"

Crawford had been watching the doctor with a taut, bleak expression on his gaunt face, and he answered in a hollow, resigned way. "No."

"Then perhaps you will reconsider my proposition."

"No," said Crawford, in that same hollow tone.

Huerta reached beneath his coat for his silver cigarette case, taking a smoke from this to fit it in the holder. He did not raise his eyes to Crawford again as he moved across the room toward the door. He pulled open the portal, and only then, turning toward Crawford, did his glance rise. Again Crawford was swept with that strange, hypnotic dizziness, as he stared into the man's eyes. It struck him as childishly melodramatic, and he wanted to laugh, and could not.

"I think you will regret coming back this morning," said Huerta, in a barely audible voice, before he turned to go out. "I think you will regret it exceedingly "

Chapter Six

"Tell Us What Happened."

AN ADOBE BANCO ran down one side of the cookshack on the inside, forming a bench, and it was upon this that Jacinto had deposited his generous bulk. He was bent in childish concentration over a block of wax from which he carefully peeled thin strips, depositing these with much care into a clay bowl. Small, intimate mutters rumbled up from him with each process.

"Ah, so," he mumbled, slicing off a piece, "ah *sí*," and sliced off another, and then jumped erect in startled surprise, dropping the block of wax. "Ah, Crawford!"

Crawford stepped on in through the door, sniffing. "Smells like bayberry."

"How—how did you get out?" quavered Jacinto, grunting painfully with the effort it cost him to stoop over and retrieve the wax.

"Nobody stopped me," said Crawford. "They gave me that upstairs bedroom, but I couldn't sleep."

"You better not come in here, Crawford," said the gross cook. "Maybe they're not watching you like they did, but you better get out of here. Why do you think Huerta kept you up at the house this morning? Didn't you see how Quartel looked at you? You're just lucky he didn't get you down here."

There was a dish of cracklings on the table, and Crawford took one, pulling a three-legged stool out to sit on it. "Quartel and the others are out chousing cattle. Making candles?"

"*Sí*," mumbled Jacinto, lowering himself back on the bench. "Nobody can make them like me. That was bayberry you smelled all right. I didn't have enough sheep tallow. First I make it into blocks and then cut it into small scraps so it melts quick without burning. I put the wax in hot water and scoop the grease off as it comes to the top. Then I strain it through a horsehair cloth to remove whatever dirt I missed in skimming. I am now heating the wax to pour in the molds. Did you ever see such fine molds? My father owned that brass one in El Paso. It holds two dozen candles at one pouring. If you came here to find out what's going on, I can't tell you."

The abrupt transition brought Crawford's head up in surprise. Jacinto set the mold end up in a dishpan, chuckling.

"I am not as stupid as I am corpulent, Crawford. You didn't come here just to eat my cracklings." His great bloodshot eyes slid upward in their pouches till they met Crawford's. "But I can't tell you anything, Crawford. I know something is going on. Huerta and that woman. Something not quite right. Tarant too, somehow. Maybe you can tell me."

"Hyacinth, what did you think of that story about Santa Anna's chests?"

"I—Santa Maria, that wax is hot." Jacinto sat shaking his finger a moment. Then he put it into his mouth. "If Santa Anna lost some chests up here, I guess he lost them, that's all. Mm, you ought to taste that bayberry. I think I'll season my *chiles rollenos* with it some time."

"You heard the one about the map?" said Crawford.

"The *derrotero? Sí,* I guess there was supposed to be a map. Isn't there always, with something like that?"

"Ever stop to think of Santa Anna's full name?"

"*Ciertamente.* Everybody knows it. Antonio Lopez de San—" Jacinto stopped, staring at Crawford. Wax dripped from the tin ladle onto the floor. Crawford popped a last crackling into his mouth.

"Would that give her a connection?" he said.

"Lopez is a common name," said Jacinto, almost defensively.

"A woman like that don't trail through this kind of country just for the scenery," said Crawford. He closed his eyes, rolling the name meditatively off his tongue. "Merida Lopez."

It must have been about then the first sound floated in from outside, the creak of saddle leather, a man's hoarse cough. Jacinto jumped across the room, jerking Crawford up out of the chair. "They're back, Crawford, you got to go, you got to get out of here, if Quartel ever gets you alone after Whitehead, he'll—"

He stopped shoving Crawford toward the doorway, and his voice faded into a series of small, choked sounds. Aforismo stood there, sweat streaking the dust in his smooth brown face, holding a belduque in his hands.

"*El amante fiel,*" he said, running his finger down the keen edge, "the Loyal Lover. Did you ever see my knife, Crawford? Truly a remarkable weapon. Handed down in my family for generations. The hilt was once studded with precious stones, but they have long since been picked out by various members of my illustrious house who were in temporary financial destitution." He took a shuffling step toward them. "Look at the *bravos* on the blade. See this one. *Nothing compares with my kiss.* Isn't that a delectable motto?"

Jacinto shrank back, staring in fascinated horror at the words cut into that side of the gleaming blade. Through the dog-run, Crawford could hear the thump of a chair in the bunkhouse, the clatter of spoons on the table.

"Please, Aforismo, please," quavered Jacinto. "Let him go. *Madre de Dios!* let him go out the door before they find him in here. You know what will happen. Quartel would—"

"And this one," Aforismo said, turning the blade over and pointing to another motto cut into that side. "This is my favorite *bravo* I think. *Tripe is sweet but bowels are better.* Don't you like that one, Jacinto?" He took another shuffling step toward them with the point almost touching Crawford's belly. "Don't you like that *bravo*, Crawford? Tell me you like it. It is my favorite, I think."

"Please, please." Jacinto was cringing behind Crawford, wringing his hands, sweat dribbling down his coarse face. "*En el nombre de Dios*, Aforismo, let him go, he never did anything to you, he never harmed one little hair of your head, I hate violence so, oh, I do hate violence so, my father he always tell me there are two sins in the world, work and fighting, and—oh, *por Dios*, Aforismo, *Santa Maria, nombre de mi madre*, let him go, let him go—"

"They say down in Durango a coyote always howls loudest in the trap," said Aforismo, nudging Crawford gently back with that needle point. "I think maybe we better all go in the bunkhouse, eh? The hands are getting hungry. Tripe is sweet but bowels are better, eh?" Crawford did not step back quickly enough, and that needle point went through his shirt with a soft ripping sound. The stinging bite of steel in the hard muscle of his belly caused his move back to be involuntary. His breath left him in a hoarse gust and he bent forward with the impulse driving through him. That was as far as it went. Aforismo's boots made that bland shuffle on the hard-packed earth, moving forward. His face twisted with frustrated anger, Crawford shifted back into the dog-run, shoving the cringing cook behind him.

"*Dios*, Aforismo, *por Dios*, no violence, please, I could not stand the sight of blood, it would make me regurgitate, please—"

Jacinto knocked over a chair backing from the dog-run into the bunkhouse. It made a loud clatter. Then Crawford was in the bunkhouse, still bent forward that way, his breath coming out harsh and swift, and he could see them. Bueno Bailey was seated at the table.

"I was just showing Crawford the *bravos* on my belduque," said Aforismo. "In Durango they say it is an ignorant man who cannot tell his sons at least one *bravo.*"

"*Bueno.*" Bailey trailed the word out in a pleased, nasal twang, shoving the bench back from the table. "Siddown, Crawford. We was just about to eat."

"I guess you never met Ford Innes, did you, Crawford," said Quartel. "This is Crawford, Ford. He is the one who brought your *amigo* back this morning."

The redheaded man in the doorway emitted a flat, harsh grunt. He must have just stepped in, for he held his saddle under one arm. The short, square lines of his body held all the lethal threat of a snub-nosed derringer. He had a flat-topped hat set squarely on his head. The bottom of his red beard was dirty from rubbing against the grease daubs on the chest of a buckskin ducking jacket with square tails that hung outside his *chivarras* and which were caught up on one side by the wooden handle of his Remington.

"Ford just got back from taking Wallace Tarant into San Antonio," said Quartel. "As many times as that shyster's been back and forth between here and town, he still can't find his way through the brush himself."

The leather rigging clattered against the hard earthen floor when Innes dropped his pack. His bushy bleached brows formed a reddish dominance above shrewd little eyes that had not left Crawford's face since he entered. He moved over and sat down across from Bailey.

"So you brought Whitehead back." His voice held the same lack of intonation as his grunt.

"Ford had been Whitehead's saddle mate for a long time," said Quartel. "I guess he'd like to know how it happened to Whitehead."

"Get us some grub, Jacinto," said Aforismo. With his belduque he indicated a place beside Bailey. "An empty seat there, Crawford. Sit down."

Crawford looked at the knife. He sat down.

The table groaned as Aforismo lowered himself onto it and put his feet on the bench, running a finger up and down his belduque. Ford Innes began playing with his spoon on the table. Jacinto came from the dog-run with a dish of beans. He fumbled the plate at the last moment and almost tipped it onto the table. His fat jowls were trembling with his chin.

"Please, please, let's not have any—"

"So Whitehead broke his neck out in the thicket," said Innes.

"Have some beans, Glenn," said Bailey, ladling them onto a plate he had shoved before Crawford.

"They call them *nacionales* down in Durango, because so many Mexicans eat them," said Aforismo. "It is said of one who is weak that he lacks *nacionales.*"

"How did it happen to Whitehead?" said Innes.

"We don't know," said Bailey, helping the man to beans. "Crawford just brought him back over his horse with his neck broke and said he found him out in the brush that way."

"How did it happen?" Innes asked Crawford.

"There was eleven shots gone from Whitehead's carbine," said Quartel.

Innes began eating in a slow, mechanical way, his jaws working steadily beneath his red beard, looking at Crawford. "Where's your iron?"

"Whitehead took away Crawford's rifle when he first came," said Aforismo.

Innes's bleached eyebrows raised, and he ceased chewing for a moment. Quartel was standing behind Crawford to one side, and Crawford caught the sly grin spreading the man's pawky lips.

"There was no other marks on Whitehead's body," Quartel said.

"Well," said Innes, still looking at Crawford that way. Finally he went back to spooning up the beans, his eyes never leaving Crawford's face. "What happened?" he said again, around a mouthful.

"Yeah." Bailey nudged Crawford on the shoulder with his spoon. "What happened?"

Crawford could hear his own breathing now. It held a harsh, driven sound. He looked from Innes to Bailey, from Bailey to Quartel, from Quartel to Aforismo. There was a patent brutal intent in all their faces. He was hunched over so far now the heat of the beans in his plate penetrated his shirt and warmed his chest.

"Where's the sorrel?" said Bailey.

"What sorrel?" said Innes.

"The horse he took out," said Quartel. "He never brought him back."

"Coffee?" It was Jacinto again, waddling in with a big pot. He set it down, looking around at the men. He wrung his great fat hands together, speaking in a small, strained voice. "Please, *señores,* please. Violence. I cannot stand it. You won't do this. Tell me you won't do this. My father, he say—"

Aforismo turned toward him, lifting the belduque. "Would you like my Loyal Lover to see inside the sack?"

"No." Jacinto backed out, lugubrious tears forming at the corners of his eyes. "No, *lástima de Dios,* tears of God, no—"

"You ain't told us what happened yet," said Innes, still eating.

"Yeah." Quartel shoved Crawford from behind. "How did you lose the sorrel? You could ride any horse I could, remember?"

Crawford's hands were clasped desperately between

his knees. There was a taut, set expression to his features. Sweat had begun trickling down his checks into his beard. His whole body was trembling.

"So you brought Whitehead in with a broken neck," said Innes.

"Yeah." Bueno poked Crawford with the spoon again. "How did it get broke?"

"Yeah." Aforismo pricked him from the other side with the knife. "What happened?"

"How did it get broke?"

"How did you lose the sorrel?"

"What happened?"

Crawford jerked away as Aforismo bent forward with that belduque again. It carried him against Bueno, sitting on his other side. Bueno pushed him back roughly. Quartel shoved him from behind so hard his chest struck the table. A small, strangled sound escaped him.

"Tell us what happened."

"*Sí*, tell us, Crawford."

"What happened, Crawford?"

"Talk, damn you." Bueno's shove was harder.

"Tell us, Crawford." The knife prick was deeper. He jerked away from it. Bailey caught him and shoved him back brutally. He made a spasmodic effort to rise. Quartel put both hands on his shoulders and forced him back down. He tried to twist around. Aforismo's belduque was in his face. He jerked back the other way into Bailey. His hands knotted and writhed between his knees underneath the table. His whole body was shuddering now.

"Where's the sorrel?"

"How'd he break his neck?"

"Talk, damn you!"

"Tell us, Crawford."

"What happened?"

"Gentlemen!" It came from the doorway, and it

stopped them abruptly. Huerta stood there, bent forward slightly, and those bluish lids were almost closed over his eyes.

"I think we all know what happened to Whitehead," he said, "don't you?" He stood there a moment, but no one answered. He dropped his eyes to the jade cigarette holder he held in one hand, tapping it to knock the ash from the cigarette, and still looking down that way, spoke again. "I think it would be wise, now, Crawford, for you to come with me, up to the house, don't you?"

Chapter Seven

SUNDAY CELEBRATION

IT WAS THE ODOR at first. Crawford lay there, staring up at the ceiling, groping up through the remnants of a sleep so heavy it left him filled with an oppressive nausea. The hangings had been removed from the bed and the four reeded mahogany posts reached up through the semi-gloom to support the bare tester frame above him. He realized where he was, then. Huerta had stopped them? Yes, Huerta had stopped them last night, and brought him to the big house to sleep. Strange, the influence Huerta had over them. Without actually doing anything. Those eyes? Maybe that was it.

Crawford sat up abruptly, the heavy chintz coverlet falling away from him. He held out his hand, staring at the fingers. They were trembling. He sniffed the air. He pulled the coverlet completely off, swinging his bare feet out of the bed. His levis were on the russet wing chair and he grabbed them up and stepped into the legs. It was that sensation again, stirring within him. It was hard for him to breathe. He sat on the bed a moment, hands clutching the covers, staring at the wall. Why? Here. Why?

He turned his head from side to side, searching the room. It was day, but the overdrapes had been pulled across the window, and he could make out the furniture only dimly in the semi-gloom. And still, down inside him, rising, growing. He bent down to pull on his boots with swift, desperate tugs, then rose. He looked like a hounded animal, the forward thrust of his rigid body imparting that narrowness to his shoulders, his eyes shifting furtively in a gaunt face. Then, on one of those shallow, indrawn breaths, it came to him, unmistakable.

Slowly, his whole body so tense it was trembling now, he turned about, sniffing. He stepped away from the bed, toward the windows, and it faded. He moved back toward the bed, and he could smell it again. With a muttered curse he bent down and tore the coverlet off. The dirty, fetid horse blanket had been laid out flat beneath the chintz spread.

"Huerta!"

It came out of him in a strangled, guttural rage, and he bent to clutch the horse blanket. He had it lifted off the bed before he released it, throwing it back down and whirling to the door. His boots made a hard thump down the stairway and into the entrance hall. He had almost passed the living-room when, through the open door, he caught sight of Huerta, seated in one of the willow chairs by the window. The doctor had been reading, and he lowered the book, leaning forward in the chair.

"You must have slept well, Crawford," he said. "It's nearly noon."

Crawford started to take a step forward, opening his mouth to speak. Then he closed it again, his fists clenched tight. There was a faint, waiting mockery on Huerta's face. Crawford whirled and stamped on out the front door. As he went down the front steps, he saw the crowd out by the corrals, and was drawn toward it. He made out Bueno Bailey and Innes among the men, but the others were new faces to him. There were half a dozen riders cavorting their horses around in the open flats, and a big Chihuahua cart was creaking out of the brush, piled high with onions and apricots and baskets of blue corn meal and squealing Mexican children and a fat Mexican peon driving. Crawford was part way across the compound when he saw the woman coming toward him. He had a momentary impulse to turn away, and stifled that. She held her heavy green satin skirt up out of the dust with one hand, and the wind ruffled the throat of her white Antoinette fichu. Her eyes, big and dark and searching, were held to his face until she reached him, and it did something to Crawford.

"They said it was a bull-tailing," she told him, coming to a stop. "I don't exactly understand."

"About the only celebration the *brasaderos* get," he said, watching her warily. "A bunch of them gather almost every Sunday somewhere to eat and drink and tail the bull. I think they're celebrating Cinco de Mayo today. Commemorating some battle at Puebla—"

He trailed off, because he could see it in her face, and he didn't particularly want to talk about the bull-tailing either. When she spoke again, her voice was husky and strained, and it must have been what was really on her mind, from the first.

"They were trying to kill you," she said. "Jacinto told me. They got you in there, and started in on you, and they meant to drive you till you cracked and fought back, and then they were going to kill you. How did you stand it so long, Crawford? Jacinto said no other man could have. Pushing you and shoving you and beating you like that. How did you stand it?"

"I'm still here, ain't I?" he said.

She drew in a breath, staring up at him. "Why did you come back with Whitehead?" she said finally. "You could have escaped."

"Maybe a man gets tired running," he said.

She caught his arm, coming in close enough for him to catch a hint of her perfume. "Crawford, I want to help you."

His whole body was rigid now, with that wariness. "I never saw a cow yet that wanted to get back inside a corral when it was outside."

"You're so suspicious," she flamed. Then she leaned toward him farther, looking up into his face. "I guess you have a right to be. You've been fighting all of them, haven't you, ever since this started. I don't blame you, Crawford. I know how you feel. I'm in the same position. I need your help as much as you need mine."

It had been a long time since a woman stood this close to him, with her hair shining like that, and her eyes. He felt a weakness seep through him. He stared at the soft red curve of her lip, and his voice was hardly audible.

"What are you talking about?"

"Have you ever heard of Mogotes Serpientes?" she said.

"Snake Thickets? I guess so. It's supposed to be somewhere west of Rio Diablo in that stretch of bad brush."

"You've never actually been there?" Her voice was tense.

"I don't know who has," he said. "There's a lot of the *brasada* nobody's ever seen, white man *or* Indian. There's a stretch due south from here just above the Rio Grande called Resaca Espantosa. Nobody's ever been through it. I don't know why they call it Haunted Swamp."

"But there is a good reason for the name Mogotes Serpientes?"

"So they say. It's supposed to be so full of snakes no man could stay alive in there more than a few—" He trailed off as he realized how far he had let her allure carry him, and pulled roughly away from her, his mouth twisting down at one corner.

"Crawford," she said, trying to get in close again. "Please. Don't. I mean it. You've got to believe me. If you believe in anything, you've got to—"

"Huerta made me a proposition too," said Crawford. "It didn't pack such a wallop, but it was along the same lines."

She flushed, stepping back from him violently. "You fool," she said, in a bitter, intense whisper. "You fool."

They were still standing that way, staring at each

other, when Huerta came out on the porch. The woman saw him and turned away, moving back toward the corrals.

"Hola, Quartel," someone over by the pens shouted. "When are you letting the *toros* out? I got a twenty-dollar pot for the first man to tail a bull."

"It's mine." Quartel's bellow came from somewhere in the crowd, and then he appeared, running in that stiff, saddle-bound stride of his toward the horses. "Aforismo, let that blue out. He ought to give us a good run."

Used to working the wild, savage cattle of the brush-land, the Mexicans trained their horses to spin away from the side on which a man mounted as soon as he lifted a foot to the stirrup. Though this saved many a *vaquero* from being gored by a ringy bull which he had just released after throwing and branding the beast, it took a good man to get on one of these horses. Each rider had a string of animals, and from his bunch Quartel had saddled a brown horse they called a *trigueño*. He knocked the reins loose of the corral post and snapped them over the *trigueño's* head. Then he checked the animal, pulling the nigh rein in till it twisted the *trigueño's* head down toward its shoulder so that the horse's action would be inhibited long enough for him to mount. As soon as Quartel raised his left foot, the *trigueño* tried to whirl, but that checking action held him long enough for Quartel to jam his foot in the stirrup and swing aboard in one violent movement. Then he released the tight rein and allowed the animal to spin toward the right.

From outside the cedar-post corral, Aforismo and several other *vaqueros* had goaded and prodded a blue bull until it was separated from the other bulls within the enclosure. As it neared the gate, Aforismo let down the drop bar.

In their natural state, running the brush, these cows were among the wildest animals of the world, and the several days this cut of bulls had spent penned up had put them in a frenzied rage. The blue stood there a moment, glaring suspiciously at the opening, pawing the ground. His great long curving horns had been scored and ripped and punched by the brush until it looked as if someone had hacked them over with a knife, and a pattern of scars formed a network across the gleaming lathered hide of his forequarters. From the side, he looked deceptively heavy, his length so extended that his back swayed, but as he lashed his tail and shifted around to display a rear view, his narrow hips and cat hams and ridgepole back became apparent. Abruptly, with a hoarse bellow, he lowered his head, and swinging it from side to side, galloped out of the gate.

Quartel yelled something, dug in with his Chihuahuas and whacked his quirt against the *trigueño's* rump at the same time. The brown horse burst into a headlong run, followed by most of the other *vaqueros,* shouting and yelling and snapping their quirts against leather *chivarras* and fancy *charro* pants. The blue bull had spotted an opening in the brush across the compound, and he shook the ground tearing for it. But the horsemen swiftly closed up on the animal. Quartel and another *vaquero* were bunched together in the lead. Quartel raked his *trigueño* with those huge Chihuahua guthooks, and the horse spurted ahead, drawing up beside the bull. Quartel leaned out of the saddle and made a grab for that lashing tail. But the blue bull jammed its forefeet into the ground and came to a jarring halt, plowing twin furrows in the earth. Quartel was several lengths on by before he could swing back in the saddle and pull his horse around; by that time the bull had turned in a half circle and cut for the brush.

The other *vaquero* had pulled up shorter than Quartel, and was in a position to run down the bull on its quarter. He was a tall, supple youth on a short-coupled horse they called a *bayo coyote,* its coat a buckskin color with a black line running down the spine, with a black mane and tail. Quartel spurred and quirted his *trigueño* in a last desperate effort to reach the bull first, but just at the edge of brush, the other *vaquero* pulled up beside the blue and leaned out to grab for that tail.

He caught its hairy end, and dallied it around his saddle horn, clapping the guthooks to his *bayo coyote* at the same time. The buckskin gave a spurt that pulled it ahead of the blue bull, and just as the horse smashed into the first thicket, the tail of the bull snapped taut, yanking its hind feet from beneath it. The *vaquero* tore the tail off his horn and hunched forward with his arm before his face all at the same time, and as he disappeared into the thicket the ground shook with the bull's falling. Huerta had come down from the house, and he moved in behind Crawford.

"I understand a good man can break the bull's neck every time," he said. "Why don't you try it, Crawford?"

Crawford's hands closed tightly, and he did not look at Huerta. The inside of his mouth was dry and cottony as he watched the *vaquero* come back through the mesquite into the open, prancing his *bayo coyote* proudly.

"You better go back to herding dogies, Quartel," the *vaquero* grinned, "and leave the grown ones to men."

"If you're a man, let's see your *reata,*" roared Quartel, wheeling his *trigueño* toward the man and unlashing his 40-foot rope from his saddle.

The rider fought his excited buckskin around in a circle as he tore his own rope from the saddle, and when he had completed the circle, the rope was free and the two riders were facing each other about a hundred yards apart.

"*Vamanos, Indita,*" shouted Quartel, his huge cart-wheel spurs gouging the brown into a headlong run toward the other man.

"Are they crazy?" said Huerta.

"Stay around the border much and you'll get used to it," Merida told him. "The *vaqueros* used to do the same thing on the rancho where I was born. They'd rather rope than eat."

"Duello," said Crawford.

"With ropes?" It caused Huerta distinct effort to evince even the dim incredulity.

"Lot of 'em would rather fight with ropes than guns," Crawford told him. "More than one lawman has been dragged to death here in the brush."

It had taken that long for the two riders to meet, passing one another not 10 feet apart. At the last moment Quartel made a pass with his rope arm. Indita's own throw caused him a hoarse exhalation that turned into a shout of triumph as he saw his loop settling over Quartel's head. Then it happened. As much as he had handled horses, Crawford did not think he had ever seen one turn so fast. One instant the *trigueño* was racing past the *bayo coyote,* the next it was facing in the opposite direction, Quartel's own involuntary grunt still hanging in the air to tell what a vicious effort he had put into the reining. The motion had carried Quartel from beneath Indita's loop in that last moment, and now he sat the *trigueño* perfectly still, facing after Indita's retreating buckskin.

Quartel's first pass had been a feint, and he still retained his rope. It was so slight a flirt of his hand that Crawford barely caught it. He did not spin the loop above his head. He tossed it underhand, the way he had thrown it with Africano in the corral. It was a hooley-ann, spinning flatly out above Indita, seeming to hover above him an instant, no bigger than the brim of his sombrero; then it was taut about his shoulders, and he was pulled over the back of his horse with a resounding thump.

"I ought to drag you for your presumption," said Quartel, shifting his horse forward so he could get enough slack in his rope to flirt it off Indita as the man rose. Then, pulling the rawhide clothesline in with a series of quick, skillful snaps, he turned the *trigueño* to prance it over toward them, grinning at Merida. "How do you like that, *señorita?*"

"I have seen it done before," said Merida.

Quartel's face darkened. "You don't think I am any good?"

"I didn't say that."

"Listen," he shouted, thumping his chest, "I am the best goddam roper in the world. I am the best goddam rider in the world. I am—"

"Don't be a boor," said Huerta, in faint disgust.

"A what?" Quartel wheeled the horse around in a growing rage, the sweat greasing his coarse face. "I'll show you." He started pounding his chest again. "I'll show you who's good. I'll make you a bet. I'll bet you a *talega* full of gold pesos that I can, blindfolded, with one end of the *reata* tied to my own neck and not to be touched by my hands, riding a bareback horse of your own choosing, forefoot each of any ten bulls we got in a pen, and break their necks."

Huerta shrugged, smiling in a faint, vague dismissal. Quartel reined the *trigueño* in closer. "I mean it," he bellowed. "Are you afraid to make the bet? Could anybody where you come from do it?"

"Frankly, I don't think anyone can do it," said Huerta, disinterestedly.

"I can," yelled Quartel. "I'm the best—"

"Don't be a fool, Quartel," the woman told him. "You'll kill yourself. One mistake with that rope around your neck and you'll be dead."

That was the final impetus. *"Hijo de la chingada,"* shouted Quartel, whirling his *trigueño* away from them. "How many bulls you got in that corral, Aforismo? Seven? Get me three more. Get me three more from that holding pen across the arroyo. I'll show you what roping really is, Merida. You're going to see a performance tonight you'll never forget!"

Chapter Eight

Best Roper in the World

THE THRONG ABOUT the large cedar-post corral was oddly subdued. Some of the *vaqueros* had dragged the blue bull over to the cooking fire for Jacinto to spit, but the gross cook had left the carcass lying on the ground. He stood with the middle bar of the fence making a deep indentation in the incredible protuberance of his stomach as the crowding *vaqueros* pressed in from behind.

"*Madre de Dios,* Crawford, why do you let him do this thing?" wailed the cook, running his fat hands nervously up and down the rail. "I don't want to see a man die."

"Then why watch?" said Crawford.

"Please, Crawford, you take such a brutal attitude. Don't you know this is the way Oro Peso died down in Mexico? He was the greatest roper in the world, Quartel's boasting to the contrary. Oro Peso used to go around making this same bet. Then somebody took him up on it. The third bull pulled him from his horse. His neck was broken like you'd snap a switch of mesquite. Please—"

"Hola, *compadres!*" shouted Quartel, from outside the corral, and they saw that he had stripped his *trigueño* of its saddle. Indita dropped the bar and Quartel trotted the animal in, laughing as the bulls bunched up on the other side, bawling. "You see, already they are afraid of me. Who is going to put the blindfold on? Merida, will you honor me?"

"Why not?" The woman's voice held a savage undertone that surprised Crawford. She caught his eyes on her and turned toward Crawford. When she saw the look on his face, she threw her head back that way, to laugh. It held a rich, wild mockery. "What's the matter, Crawford? Don't you like that in a woman? Maybe you haven't known the right women."

Still laughing, she reached through the bars to tie the bandanna behind Quartel's head as the man slipped off the *trigueño* and turned his back to her. Then he swung aboard again, and tied one end of the rope he was carrying about his thick neck in a noose, too small to slip over his head. Merida's face was flushed excitedly as she watched him prance the *trigueño* away, and her eyes flashed in frank anticipation. Huerta pulled out his cigarette case and put a smoke into his jade holder. His motions were as languid as ever, but Crawford thought his fingers pinched the holder more tightly than was necessary.

"Hola!" shouted Quartel, wheeling his *trigueño* in the middle of the corral and kicking its flanks with his heels. The horse charged toward the bulls, and the animals strung out along the fence. Quartel was an uncanny judge of distance; when his horse was but half a length from the fence, he made a quarter turn and raced along the bars after the last bull in the running bunch.

"*Andale!*" yelled the man, and made his toss.

The loop snaked about the forefeet of that last bull as it turned at the corner of the corral, and as Quartel felt the rope snap taut, he let go completely with his hands, pulling his thick neck down into his shoulders to set it and jerking back with his torso at the last moment. The bull turned a flip, its shoulder striking the rump of the running animal in front, and as the falling bull struck, Quartel shoved his reins hard against the *trigueño's* neck to wheel inward and give himself slack on the rope. He clutched for the slackening rawhide and sent a flirt down the rope that lifted the loop off the bull's forelegs, and when he turned away, he was pulling the line in.

"*Viva Quartel, viva!*" shouted the *vaqueros,* shoving Crawford up against the fence with their shifting press and deafening him with their cheers. Grinning, Quartel kicked the *trigueño* after the bulls again. It started them off once more, bawling and running. Quartel's hearing was as uncanny as his judgment of distance; he rode with his head lifted, and when a scarred brindle bull broke from the others, running along the fence and cutting across the middle of the corral, Crawford could see Quartel's head turn after the animal. The Mexican reined his *trigueño* over that way, kicking it into a dead run that closed the space between himself and the bull in a swift instant.

"*Ahora,*" he shouted, "now," and tossed. His rope caught the bull's hind feet instead of its forefeet, and as a strange sighing sound rose from the crowd, Quartel must have sensed something was wrong, for he spurred the *trigueño* brutally, and its frenzied leap into a headlong run gave him slack enough in the rope for that last moment to send a flirt down its length that carried the loop off the bull's hind feet before it could draw closed. The bull stumbled into the other animals as they turned the corner and milled down this side of the corral. By that time Quartel had his rope coiled, and he maneuvered the bawling, excited animals so that they strung out down the fence once more, and then ran his horse up behind the last one. This time it was the forefeet, and he dropped the animal, breaking its neck as before. The end of the rope about Quartel's neck was not a slip noose, but Crawford could see the rawhide dig into the thick brown flesh of Quartel's neck as he jerked back, till the skin showed a white ridge above and below the lasso. He watched in undeniable fascination as the Mexican flirted in the rope and turned his horse after them once more. Shouting, Quartel closed the gap between himself and another bull and made his toss. He released the lasso with his hand as soon as it was in the air. The instant that loop caught on the running bull's forefeet, Quartel reined his *trigueño* in a quarter turn that wheeled it away from the running bull. The bull's own forward motion would draw the noose tight about its legs, and the turning maneuver of the horse would stretch the rope taut between them as soon as that noose was completely closed. In that instant, with the bull hitting the end of the rope and flipping, Quartel had to wheel his horse back or be pulled off. He had already turned the *trigueño* away from the bull, and the noose was making its singing sound closing on those churning forefeet, when a big *hosco golondrino* cut away from the other animals running along the fence and turned out into the corral, directly across the head of the *trigueño*. Quartel's huge neck sank into his shoulders, and he put the reins against the *trigueño's* neck to swerve it back as he felt the rope snapping taut. But the turn would have run the horse head-on into the *hosco golondrino*. It was the first time Crawford had seen that *trigueño* fight the bit; its head turned in and its neck arched, it lurched in the opposite direction from Quartel's reining.

"Crawford," screamed Merida, and then the full weight of the falling bull hit the end of that rope with Quartel going in the wrong direction to take the shock. He made a small, choked sound as he was snapped off the *trigueño's* rump. Crawford was not conscious of going through the bars. He found himself on the inside of the corral, with someone climbing through the rails on his left. He did not realize who it was till he had started running toward Quartel where he was rolling across the ground. Then from the corner of his eye, Crawford caught the white flutter of Merida's fichu.

"Get back, you crazy fool," he screamed at her, diving headlong at her as a couple of crazed bulls charged by. He struck her with his arms around her waist and carried her back against the bars as a third animal crashed past where she had been standing. He rolled to his feet, leaving her there huddled up against the fence, and dodged through another pair of the bawling, frenzied animals, coughing in the dust.

The bull Quartel had thrown was scrambling to its feet, the *reata* still caught around one foreleg. Crawford saw the slack rope hiss taut as the animal broke into a stumbling gallop, and knew he could never reach it in time. If Quartel's neck were not already broken, his head would be pulled from his body now. Another bull went past behind Crawford, its shoulder sending him spinning, and he threw himself bodily toward the rope where it lay tautening across the ground, in a last desperate effort to try and get it before the bull had stretched it completely.

But even as he did so, he saw Quartel had risen to his hands and knees. Still blindfolded, the man must have heard the sing of the rope and known what was occurring. He gave his head one dazed shake and jumped to his feet, sinking his neck in that way and throwing himself backward. His body was at a three-quarter angle when the rope snapped taut; he would have fallen completely if the line had not caught him. The impetus of his jerking back that way and the weight of his body combined to upset the bull once more. The ground shuddered to the falling animal. Crawford heard the crack of its broken neck.

"How's that, Huerta?" laughed Quartel, running forward to slacken the rope so he could flirt the loop free. "I told you I wouldn't pull on it by hand. Did you see that? I didn't touch it with my hands, did I? I'll bet you never saw a roper could do that down around Mexico City. Even Oro Peso. Did you think I was finished? Not with a neck like that. I could throw ten bulls all at once. Where's my horse? Bring me that *trigueño*. I'm not through yet. Not with a neck like that."

In a daze, Crawford picked himself off the ground, seeing Indita run out to corner the *trigueño* and lead him over to the sweating, roaring Quartel. Stumbling back to the fence, Crawford watched the whole crazy performance begin once more. It was a nightmare of shouting *vaqueros* and bawling bulls and singing ropes and clouds of acrid russet dust obscuring the whole pattern every time the animals broke into a run. Quartel took three casts to nail the seventh bull, and it was obvious he was tiring.

"Three more," Crawford heard Jacinto mumbling beside him. "Three more. Oh, *madre de Dios,* let him get over with this, will you, and I'll never forget to say my rosary again. Three more, three more—"

Two more. One more. "Hola!" shouted the Mexican, *"ahora,"* and the rope spun, and caught, and tautened, and the ground shook as the last bull broke its neck. Coiling in the rope, Quartel spurred the *trigueño* to the gate, ripping off his blindfold. They were all running that way, Aforismo catching the man as he slid off the lathered, quivering horse, pounding him on the back. Even Merida had lifted her skirts to run that way, drawn by the excitement. Quartel came through the crowd, sweating and grinning and pounding himself on the chest with his hairy fist. "I told you. The best roper in the world. What do you think of it, Huerta? Have you ever seen better? Was Oro Peso better?" Then a thought seemed to strike him, and he sobered, looking around at the *vaqueros.* "When I was pulled off the horse. Someone was in the corral. I heard them."

The hubbub sank until there was only the muffled sound of stirring bodies, and Quartel saw the direction their glances had taken, one after another. He stared at Crawford in disbelief.

"You—"

Crawford shrugged, sullenly. "It was automatic, I guess. I didn't think."

"Yes." Huerta allowed twin streamers of gray smoke to escape his nostrils. "I wonder what would have happened if you had stopped to think."

Crawford flushed, turning toward him, but Quartel came forward, clapping his hand on Crawford's shoulder. "Huerta, I'm surprised at you. After all, he saved my life. And how about you. A *talega* of pesos."

"I made no wager," said Huerta, tapping ash from his cigarette.

The blood swept into Quartel's face, and he stepped forward to grab the lapels of Huerta's coat with one huge hand, jerking the man toward him. "Huerta, I bet you a *talega* of pesos—"

"I made no wager." Huerta had not moved his hands. One of them still held the cigarette holder at his side; the other rested in the pocket of his coat. But he was looking into Quartel's eyes, and his own eyes had opened wider. The veined dissolution of his heavy bluish lids had lifted until the whole pupil was visible.

"That's right, that's right," said Jacinto nervously. "Huerta didn't take up your bet, Quartel. You was so busy shouting and all you didn't wait to see if he'd made the bet with you."

"If he had, he'd pay me," said Quartel, still looking into Huerta's eyes, an indefinable puzzlement drawing a faint furrow through his brow, and something else. Abruptly he turned around, raising his voice. "*Caramba,* if I ain't going to get a *talega* of pesos, I should get some kind of reward. You don't see a rodeo like that every day. How about it, Merida? I want a reward—"

He had shoved through the crowd toward her, catching her around the waist. Apparently not divining his intent at first, she had been smiling, her face still flushed with that excitement. But as he caught her and bent his face to hers, the smile twisted into a grimace. She threw her forearm across his neck and tried to lever him away.

"Vayase con la música a otra parte," she cried, anger causing her to break into Spanish. *"Tu barrachon, largo de aquí, tu chile, no puedo sufrir su insolencia—"*

"My insolence?" laughed Quartel, grasping her wrist and tearing it from between them. The force of it drew a gasp of pain from Merida; she began writhing more violently in his embrace, and tried to scratch his face with the other hand. But he caught that too, and forced both her hands behind her until he had her wrists crossed with his arms about her waist. In that last moment, he quit grinning. Crawford had seen the same expression in the man's face before, when he looked at Merida, but never so palpable, never so clearly recognizable. His voice came from deep in his throat, husky and sensual and demanding.

"Besame, querida," he said, and lowered his sweating face to hers.

"Let her go, Quartel!"

The Mexican stopped, with his lips not quite touching Merida. The woman's body ceased to writhe; she stood there in his arms, bent backward like a bow, looking up at him. Without releasing her, Quartel raised his head and turned it over his shoulder till he could see Crawford. It had taken Crawford that long to get through the laughing, shouting crowd; they were no longer making any noise, and they had spread away from him. He stood there with his boots spread a little on the hard-packed dirt and the weight of his shoulders thrown forward, the bitter intensity of his face only accentuating its gauntness.

"Oh." The word came out softly, slyly on Quartel's breath. "Maybe you'd rather be the one to kiss her. First he saves my life, then he wants to take my woman away."

"Your woman?" gasped Merida.

"Take your hands off, damn you—"

"Don't swear at me, Crawford." The hurt tone of Quartel's voice held that pawky mockery. "I thought we were *amigos*. I thought you saved my life in the corrals."

"Quartel—"

"*Si?*" The man had released Merida and wheeled to face Crawford. For a moment he stood there, his heavy chest rising and falling gently with his breathing. The mockery faded from his face, leaving a heavy, deliberate intent. His shift to the side was unhurried, but Crawford's effort to keep facing the man came in a swift, spasmodic reaction. Then Quartel stood there again. "Nobody swears at me, Crawford," he said, and then, moving with incredible speed for such a bulky man, he leaped forward. Crawford had been waiting for something, but it came so fast his move to block it was aborted. Quartel had him by the shoulders, knocking him off balance, and Crawford had to stumble backward to keep from falling. "Do you understand that?" Quartel was shouting it now, hoarsely, allowing his ebullience to escape finally. "I'm *amansador,* here, I'm foreman, and nobody swears at me or tries to stop me whatever I'm doing. I rod this outfit and I can do anything I want and nobody can stop me, do you hear?"

It was then Crawford realized what he had brought up against. Stumbling backward, he had lurched into the *trigueño* and it had kept him from falling. He was held against it now by Quartel's hands gripping his shoulders. The animal heat of it penetrated through his shirt, and something else clawed at him, somewhere way down in his vitals.

In a new spasm, Crawford tried to lurch free of Quartel's grip; but the man had still managed to keep him off balance, and he was held there, with his knees bent and his body pushed off to one side so that he had no leverage. He was shoved back hard against the horse again, and the hot, living, hairy, animal resilience of it against his back intensified that vague alarm inside him.

"Do you hear me, Crawford, do you hear me—"

Quartel's voice came through to him as if the man were far away. Crawford was writhing from side to side, trying to escape, but he was still held at that disadvantage. He had his hands on the man's arms, tearing at them. The effort rocked Quartel from side to side, but failed to loosen his grip. Crawford's face was twisted, and he was gasping hoarsely, because it was growing in him now, raking at him insistently with its subtle, insidious nails. His legs were beginning to tremble and the muscles across his belly were twisting up into little involuntary knots.

"Let go, let go—"

The violent movement and their shouting had excited the horse, and it began to shift around behind Crawford. It had been standing there against the fence where Quartel left it when he slid off. Crawford had it pinned up against the bars, and the animal whinnied nervously, trying to get from between him and the fence. Aforismo moved from the crowd to grab the *trigueño's* reins and pull its head down.

"What's the matter, Juarez?" he said. "Crawford, don't do that, you're spooking this horse."

"Yeah, quit shouting!" roared Quartel. "Can't you see what you're doing to my *trigueño?* Hasn't he been through enough today? Quit jumping around like that."

He realized what they were doing. That had been the intent in Quartel's face. It didn't help him now to understand. Nothing helped him now. It had its grip on him. His struggles had become a blind, frenetic effort to escape. Not from Quartel, now. It was the horse. The shrill sound of the *trigueño's* whinny and the rising turbulence of the beast's nervous movement against him drove Crawford to a new violence in his attempts at escape. It was no longer small or vague in him. It filled his whole consciousness. It spread through his legs and lower body in a clutching, stabbing pain that caused his knees to tremble and jerk. It filled his chest with a terrible constriction. And as before, the pain was rapidly turning to something else.

"Let go, damn you, let go—"

He was screaming it now, in animal panic, his face contorted, his whole body writhing and struggling in a blind frenzy that only excited the horse further. He felt it rear up, and would have fallen backward beneath it had not Aforismo yanked it down hard with his grip on the reins. The hot hide was wet with nervous sweat against Crawford's back, and he could feel the ripple of its muscle with every movement it made, and every ripple sent a new wave of panic through him. All reason was gone from his mind and he was sinking into a dark vortex of that terrible panic like a cow sinking into a black bog.

"What's the matter, Crawford? Are you afraid of the horse?"

"Let go, please, for God's sake, let go."

"What's the matter, Crawford?"

"Leggo, leggo, leggo—"

He stopped screaming. It took him a long time to comprehend he was no longer being held against the horse. He crouched there on his knees where he had fallen when Quartel had stepped back, releasing him. The movement of the animal behind him raised a flurry of dirty brown dust. Coughing in it, Crawford stared up at Quartel. The rage had disappeared from Quartel's face. His lips were spread in that pawky smile.

"Sure," he said, "I'll let you go. What will you do if I

let you go?"

Aforismo had pulled the *trigueño* out from behind him now, and Crawford crouched there on his hands and knees, black hair falling dankly over his feverish eyes. He looked like a trapped animal, his breath escaping him in hoarse gasps, his head turning in quick jerks as his wild glance leaped from one person to another. First it was Merida. There was a desperate plea in the way she bent toward him, her bosom rising and falling, her red lower lip dropped away from the shadowed white line of her teeth, glistening damply. Then Huerta, managing to convey a bored amusement without actually expressing anything in his face, as he studied Crawford distantly. And Jacinto, great, lugubrious globules of sweat sliding down his brown face, wringing his fat hands, making small, unintelligible sounds of pain.

A vagrant anger swept Crawford and he tried to collect it and hold it in him, bitter and acrid and violent. But it held no strength, and a shift of the wind swept the fetor of the *trigueño* to him once more, and the anger disappeared. There was none of the spasm of panic now. It was heavy and oppressive in him, holding him down like a physical weight, robbing him of all resolve, dominating all other emotion. He was still shaking violently, and the salty tears blinded him. He felt a dim impulse to move twitch at his legs, and he knew a moment there when he thought he could rise. Then he heard the guttural, frustrated sound he made, and knew he was still on the ground, and felt an overpowering impulse to give way and cry.

"I thought so," said Quartel, and turned to take the reins from Aforismo. He checked the animal to prevent its whirling away from him, and jumped onto its back. He released the rein, and the *trigueño's* head came around with a snap as it spun to trot off toward the fires.

The other *vaqueros* followed one by one, in an uncomfortable silence. Huerta patted a yawn.

"They've got some cane chairs over under those coma trees," he said. "I think I'll watch the proceedings from there. Coming, Merida?"

She did not answer. She was looking at Crawford, her face pale. Huerta shrugged, moved languidly across the dusty compound. Then it was just the two of them, with Crawford finally gaining his feet, unable to meet her eyes. Merida's weight had settled back onto her high heels slowly. That ripe lower lip had contracted against her teeth till her mouth was twisted across them faintly. Her husky voice was barely audible.

"I had hoped Huerta was wrong."

He stared at her, wanting to turn and run, unable to, somehow, and finally it came from him, guttural, hardly recognizable. "Whadda you mean?"

"About that fellow in the mine," she said.

"Whaddaya mean?" Had that been him? Shrill, and cracked, like that?

"You know what I mean," she said. "Not only pain. Fear. And not only fear of what originally caused the pain."

"No—"

"Yes!" she said thinly. "Yes! It's not just the horses any more. It's everything. You're a coward, Crawford. You're a coward!"

Chapter Nine

STILL IN THE THROES OF FEAR

THE GIRANDOLE CANDELABRA on the mantel looked like a brooding ghoul in the evening gloom which shrouded the living-room of Otis Rockland's house. The French windows at the front extended completely to the floor, double-hung sashes forming the upper half, paneled gates of unpolished oak being the lower section. The damask hangings had been pulled across during the afternoon to shut out the sun, but the windows themselves were partly ajar, allowing the sounds from the corrals to enter the room. Someone was playing a guitar over there where they were still roasting the bulls that had been killed. A woman's laugh came dimly.

Crawford raised his head a moment where he sat in a willow chair by the window; then he lowered it once more into his hands. His face was bleak and empty. He did not know how long it was since he had come here, unable to face them out there.

When the creak of the porch came mutedly to him, he gave no sign. Then there was more sound, louder, more recognizable. His head lifted as the noise terminated with a muffled crash.

"Crawford!"

Just once like that, shrill and cracked. He got to his feet and ran to the door, tearing it open. It was the side table in the entrance hall which had made the crash. Merida must have pulled it over, falling. The marble top had smashed, and a piece of it lay on the floor beside her. The front door stood open wide.

"Merida?" he said, dropping to one knee. "You fell?"

"No." She stirred feebly, rising to one elbow with his

help, hanging her head over against his knee a moment. The kitchen door opened, and her maid padded down the hall in bare feet, a small, wizened Indian, so dark she looked negroid, dressed in nothing more than a white cotton shift.

"It's all right, Nexpa," Merida told her. "A little accident. Crawford will help me to my room."

She allowed him to help her up the stairs, leaning heavily on his arm. The warmth of her body flowed through Crawford, and when they reached the second floor he was breathing heavily. Beyond the last step, Merida pulled away from him, her eyes meeting his in a swift, unreadable way.

She turned and moved toward her room, halting a moment outside Huerta's closed door, as if listening. Then she opened the door of her bedroom. He had kept from asking by an effort, but now he followed her in hesitantly, speaking.

"Huerta came up?"

She closed her door softly. "He wasn't at the corrals when I left."

"Maybe he got hungry for his red beans." Her face lifted to him, eyes widening, and he shrugged. "Jacinto said something about dope."

She pursed her lips, moving around him toward the table. "Couldn't you see it? Opium when we were in Mexico City. Peyote now."

"Those beans."

"Yes. You've heard it. The Indians call it *raíz diabólica*. Devil weed. They've been using it for centuries in Mexico. Even the Aztecs knew of it. They called it peyotl. It's effect isn't as marked as opium. He seems capable of eating those beans all day. They make a drink of it that's more potent."

"He said something about a complaint," Crawford told her.

Her mouth twisted somewhat. "Maybe he has an old wound. He's been around. He'd take dope anyway. That's just the kind he is. You saw the kind. Dissolute? I don't know. Whatever you want." She had got a punk off the table and was lighting the candles in the porcelain candelabra supported by oak wall brackets. Then she saw how he was looking at her, and turned part way. "What is it?"

He looked away. "Nothing."

She caught his arm, turning him back.

"No," she said. "It is something. Huerta?"

Crawford pulled away from her hand, uncomfortable, somehow. "I just can't see you with him. You're not the type."

"What type do you think I am?"

He started to answer. Then he moved his shoulders again, letting out a muted, rueful sound. "I guess I don't know, really, do I?"

"Don't you?" She was meeting his glance with a wide, candid demand in her eyes.

"Santa Anna's chests?" he said.

She drew in a long, slow breath, and nodded, finally. "You do know, then," she murmured, almost inaudibly. "You have known, all along." She hesitated, studying him. When she spoke again, her voice was stronger. "That's inconceivable to you, isn't it?"

"No—"

"Yes!" She blew out the punk with the word. "You've lived in the *brasada* most of your life. Money to you represents no more than a barren, lonely ranch like this and a herd of cattle to support it. You have no conception of what riches can really mean. Not just the horses, the servants, the jewels. The grace, Crawford, the ease, the beauty, the way of life." An intensity had gripped her voice, and her face was flushed. "Do you know what it is to be a peon in Mexico? No. You've never seen it, have you? You've seen the women in the brush here, living like animals in a one-room mud house with nothing but a cotton sheet for a dress. That's nothing. They're rich. They're hidalgos compared with a real peon. I should know. I was one, Crawford. I won't be one again. I'd rather steal and lie and cheat. I'd rather murder. Can you understand that? I will, if it's necessary. I—"

She broke off, breathing deeply, looking wide-eyed up at him. Then a short bitter laugh escaped her, and she turned away, the line of her shoulders bowing faintly. Light drew a soft glow from the rich black hair drawn tightly across the back of her head. With a new understanding of the woman, he stepped in behind her.

"All right," he said.

The simple acceptance of that drew her around. They were standing so close her breast touched his when it stirred faintly to her breathing.

"You were going to tell me what happened downstairs," he murmured.

"Derrotero?" she said, watching his face narrowly.

It was an effort to keep it expressionless. "The map?"

"It's why Huerta wanted to keep you here in the first place," she said. "Quartel and Tarant were against it, but Huerta thought you had some reason for coming here. He was right, Crawford. Nothing else could make you take what they've been doing. You've got part of the *derrotero,* and you think one of us has the rest. Well, one of us has!"

She turned around and did something with the waist of her dress, beneath the fichu. When she turned back, she held a piece of torn, yellowed paper in her hand.

"There are three pieces to the map," she said. "This is one of them."

"Lopez?" he asked.

"Yes," she muttered. "Santa Anna had many wives. My

mother was one. You will recall that the captain of the mule train sent one third of the map to Santa Anna himself. It was about all my mother got out of Santa Anna's estate when he died."

"Who was it downstairs?" he asked.

"He came from behind. It was dark. I did not see."

He stared at the section of paper a long time, scratching his dirty beard with a thumbnail. "Huerta's been trying to find out all along if I have the *derrotero*. The fact that he doesn't know for sure has kept him from making any definite move, one way or another. What would he do if he found out, for sure, one way or another?"

"Why should he find out?" she said.

"You're with Huerta."

"Am I?" she said, moving in close again. "Maybe I *was*."

"You tried that before," he said.

"No," she said hotly. "Will you never trust me, Crawford? I want to help you. Not just the map. That doesn't matter, now. Out there, with the *trigueño*. I'm sorry for what I called you."

"Maybe you were right," he said, bitterly.

"No! You're not a coward, intrinsically. Can't you see what they were doing? Maybe Huerta was the first to see how it was—about your legs. Now they all know. They're using it, Crawford. Quartel used it today. He shoved you up against the horse and held you there till you were half-crazy with panic. He knew you wouldn't fight him in that state. It wasn't fear of him that demoralized you. It was horrible to watch." She reached up to grasp his elbows with her hands, lifting her weight toward him. "But I've seen what you used to be, too. When you brought Whitehead back. No coward could have done that. Come back, with Whitehead that way, knowing what you would have to face, here. Do you realize what it did to me? To come out on the porch that morning and see you standing there beside Whitehead's body, knowing what it meant. It doesn't happen to a person often in her life, Crawford. That sort of feeling. Let me help you, Crawford. I want to. I can't if you don't trust me."

She was up against him now, almost sobbing it, and his hands had slid around her waist, the flesh hot and silken against his palm through her gown. For one last moment he tried to fight it. But he had fought so long, so alone, without anyone, and the warm resilience of her body against him filled Crawford with a giddy weakness.

"Merida," he muttered thickly, bending her back, "Merida—"

She pulled away, her face flushed. "I can't—if you don't trust me—"

He held her that way, breathing heavily, her back arched away from him by the pressure of her hands against his chest. He searched her wide, dark eyes, and found no guile there. Still filled with that desire and driven by it, he made a guttural, inarticulate sound, releasing her, and took one step to the bed, lowering himself on the embroidered muslin coverlet. He bent to take off his right Justin. The fancy stitching across the top of the boot unknotted, and he pulled it away from half a dozen eyelets in the leather, revealing a double thickness which formed a pocket.

"Used to keep my money here," he said, pulling out the piece of parchment Rockland had given him. The woman's hand trembled as she took it from him, laying it on the bed beside her piece, fitting them together. Then her pale finger crossed the map until it reached a word printed on his section. Her voice was no more than a whisper.

"Mogotes Serpientes."

"Yeah," he said, watching her. "Yeah. I never got around to using the map. Kenmare was on my tail a lot since I left San Antonio. I didn't take too much stock in the story anyway. Del never told me anything about it, and it was his uncle supposed to have been captain of that mule train. How did Rockland get hold of this portion?"

"Delcazar's uncle escaped to Mexico City, where he died, his effects being turned over to the family lawyer down there," she said. "Rockland originally wanted the Delcazar land up here for the water. He sent Tarant down to Mexico City to make sure there was nothing in the Delcazar papers which would prevent having clear title to the land when he got hold of it. Tarant found this part of the chart when he was going through those papers." She straightened slowly, allowing her gaze to reach his face. "Do you know who has the other piece, Crawford?"

"No," he said.

Her eyes grew blank; and he stood swiftly, grasping her hand. "I've trusted you, Merida. Now you've got to trust me. I don't know."

"It's got to be more than trust now," she said. "We're in it together, Crawford. If I'm to help you, you've got to help me. Will you?"

"Haven't I proved that?" he said, trying to pull her toward him with that hand. "Anything, Merida—"

She held back, calculation hardening the planes of her face. "Perhaps I should have said, *can* you?"

Just the feel of her wrist in his fingers that way, soft and satiny, started it up again in him, and he quit trying to pull her in, and took a step in toward her. "What horse you on now?"

"I mean, maybe you can't. Maybe you're incapable of it. You can't do much the way you are now, Crawford. You're only half a man. It's not just the horses any more.

It's your whole life. Everything you do is affected by it. I've thought of trying to get you a gun. A dozen times. It would be hard, but I might be able to do it. To stay unarmed here, like this—" She put her free hand against his chest to stop him. "What good would it do, Crawford? If you'd had a gun, would you have used it today? Quartel carries one. Would you have pulled yours on him?"

No woman had ever affected him so violently before. Hardly aware of what she was saying, the blood pounding through his head, he sought to force her hand aside and bend his face to hers, wanting only to feel her against him again.

"Merida," he said, the blood so thick in his throat it made him sound strangled, "I told you—anything—"

She took a deep, ragged breath, and he could not tell whether she was fighting him or herself, now. "No, Crawford. It wouldn't be any different with a gun. Not the way you are now. A gun wouldn't do you any more good than your bare hands. Quartel wanted you to fight him with your hands. You wouldn't even do that. Nothing will do you any good until you can step on a horse again without feeling that pain in your legs—that fear." She forced herself away, saying it in a cold tone, "Africano?"

It was like throwing ice water on a fire. All his ardor disappeared before the abrupt clutch of fear that word engendered in him. He stiffened for a moment, still holding that one hand. Then he dropped it and stepped back, his mouth twisted. Just the word, like that. Just the name.

"Yes." The heavy rise and fall of Merida's breast abated as she studied him, the candor gone from her face now, a cold, critical speculation filling her eyes as she studied him. "Perhaps I was wrong, Crawford. Perhaps you can't help me. Perhaps I can't help you."

"No? Let me show you," he said desperately.

Chapter Ten

Flight From Snake Thickets

THIS TIME OF NIGHT did strange things to the brush. The moon had not yet risen enough to light fully the trails winding their secretive way through the jealous' chaparral, and what vague dim light did seep through the gloom held a reflected, synthetic quality. Most of the *vaqueros* were in a drunken stupor when Crawford and the woman left the house, getting one of Rockland's prized copperbottoms and a pinto mare from the corrals without being detected. They rode north from the spread, following one of the ancient game traces which the *vaqueros* used when working the cattle. In the eerie illumination, the berries ripening on the granjeno bushes formed yellow shadow patches against the velvet backdrop of darkness farther back, and the white filament of the horse-maimer was turned to a sick erubescence where it crouched on a stony ridge. Crawford caught the dim glow of the cactus's silky blossoms, and pulled his reins in a hard jerk against the pinto's neck. The animal shied to the right, away from the horse-maimer.

"Crawford!"

The woman said it softly from behind him, a controlled anger in her voice. She moved the copperbottom up beside him, peering at his face.

"It's all right," he said impatiently.

"Crawford," she said again, in that low, insistent tone.

He tried to relax his legs against the pinto. Just a walk, and they were like that. He felt his shirt sticking to his armpits and knew the sweat was showing on his face. That terrible frustration was biting at him.

"I told you it was all right," he said harshly.

A savagery entered her voice, struggling with that restraint. "Will you quit trying to hide it, Crawford. From me. From yourself. I know all about it now. I've seen it. There's no use being ashamed of it with me. It's there. We both recognize it. Admit it. That's the first thing you've got to do."

"All right. I'm afraid. Every time it moves. Every time it bats an eyelash. Every time it—"

He stopped, realizing how violent the release had been, and it seemed the mocking echoes of his voice were dying down the sombrous lanes of the brush. He turned away from her, feeling a new wave of shame.

"That's better than nothing," she said. The tone of Merida's voice made him turn back to her. She must have been waiting for that, because the movement brought his eyes around to hers. "When you wouldn't meet Quartel back at the bull-tailing," she said, "I condemned you for being a coward. I'll never do it again. You may be afraid, but I'll never condemn you for it. The only thing I'll condemn you for is refusing to face your fear."

He felt his legs relaxing slightly, and for a moment the beat of his heart diminished. He had never talked with anyone about it like this before. He had kept it locked within himself, refusing to look at it, refusing to admit it even to himself.

"Do your legs hurt now?" she said.

"A little." His voice was tight.

"Crawford—"

"All right. A lot. They hurt like hell. I hurt all over. Does that satisfy you?"

"This the river?" she said.

He pulled the pinto to a stop and stepped off stiffly. He stood there a moment with his face into the horse, trembling faintly. When he moved away from the animal, the nebulous pain subsided somewhat in his loins.

Yet the animal's very proximity kept the irritation in his consciousness. When he pulled the map from his shirt, his hand twitched spasmodically, and he almost tore the paper. She took the paper from his uncertain hands, moving into the best of the bizarre light. They had ridden north in order to strike the Nueces River where the route on his portion of the *derrotero* started. The woman hunkered down on the ground, spreading the paper out. There was something wild about her figure, crouching there like that, her dark head brooding over the chart. She looked up abruptly. It caused him to make a small, involuntary movement, realizing how he had been watching her. He squatted down beside her, seeing the scarlet tip of her finger descend to the words printed in Spanish at one end of the chart.

"Montezuma Embrujada?"

"Yeah," he said. "You can see them right across the river. I don't know why they're called the Haunted Ruins. It's just an old Spanish fort they had here to guard the gold trains coming from the San Saba Mines."

Her finger moved down the line on the paper to the next spot. "Chapotes Platas."

"Silver Persimmons. A bunch of persimmon trees growing about five miles south of here that look silver in the moonlight. I been by there sometimes chousing cattle with Delcazar."

"Tinaja de la Tortuga." Her finger had passed on to the third spot marked on the upper portion of the map.

"Turtle Sink, we call it," he said. "There's the biggest old granddaddy turtle you ever saw living there, but I never saw any water."

"Veredas Coloradas— "

"You got me now," he said. "I told you nobody's seen all of the *brasada*. Delcazar knows more about it than anybody else I ever knew, but he can't tell me where Snake Thickets are, or what's in Lost Swamp."

"This is still on the portion of the map you had," she said.

He nodded. "It's new brush to me and thicker'n heel flies in spring. It takes a machete to get through."

Her finger was trailing on down the line, crossing the jagged tear in the paper, marking the spots noted on the second portion of the *derrotero*. "Llano Sacaguista, Puenta Piedra, Resaca Perdida—you don't know any of these?"

He shook his head. "I told you. I've never been down that way. I've heard of some. Puenta Piedra, for instance. There's supposed to be a natural stone bridge somewhere along the Rio Diablo. And most everybody in the brush has heard the tales about Lost Swamp."

"Puenta Piedra is beyond that thick brush," she said. "Why not skirt that section of the *brasada* until we strike Rio Diablo? If Puenta Piedra is somewhere along Rio Diablo, we should find it by following the river's course. Then maybe we can follow the chart from Puenta Piedra on down to the Snake Thickets."

"We won't get back before daylight," he said.

"I don't care." She rose with a toss of her head. "Let them know we've been hunting the chest. I told you there wasn't any time left to beat about the bush."

"And what have we got when we do reach Snake Thickets?" he said.

"Don't ask me!" She seemed to allow herself full release for the first time. Her face was flushed and she swung aboard the copperbottom viciously. "All I know is I can't sit around that house and wait for something to happen. The only way to find something is to go out and hunt for it—"

She stopped, as she saw him standing there staring at the pinto. It had a little roan in its black coloring which caused the dark spots to run over into the white patches, giving a sloppy, splotched effect. It stirred faintly, snorting. Merida saw what that did to him.

"Crawford—"

There was a plea in her voice. She sat quiescent, waiting. His lips flattened against his teeth. He moved slowly to the pinto, standing there, staring at the sweaty saddle. The smell of it grew in his nostrils. He was filled with the impulse to turn and run. His body twitched with it.

"Crawford—"

He put his foot in the stirrup and stepped aboard.

Silver Persimmons, Turtle Sink, Rio Diablo. They were names on the chart. They were spots in the *brasada*. They were names in his head and their reality blended with black letters on faded parchment. He lost all sense of time. His only consciousness was of movement. No telling how long it took them from Haunted Ruins to Silver Persimmons. The weird brush floated past in a sea of mingled pain and trembling and sweating. The stark arms of chaparral supplicated the night on every side. The *cenizo's* ashen hue had turned a sick lavender from recent rain, and it reeled biliously into vision and out again. Then Chapotes Platas were gleaming like newly minted coin beneath the risen moon. The woman talked sometimes, watching Crawford, in a low, insistent way.

"My mother was the *curandera* of the village. You have no idea how many plants those herb-women can make medicine from. On Saturday we would go to the river a mile away and gather herbs. I used to enjoy that. It was as far away from home as I got. The rest was mostly work. Nothing very nice to remember. Choking to death in the fumes of the herbs my mother had cooking constantly in the big brass kettle in our jacal. Rubbing my eyes all day in the smoke. She was stone blind from that. Grinding corn on the metate. I must have spent half my waking hours with that metate. Do you blame me for marrying Capitán Mendoza when he asked? I didn't love him. He was brutal and ugly. But he was stationed in Mexico City. I was fourteen at the time—"

Turtle Sink ceased to be inked words on yellowed paper and rose abruptly from the shadowed depths of the brush—a stony water hole with sand white as bleached bones 'covering its bottom and the scarred, mottled shell of a huge turtle barely visible in the black shadow beneath one end. They were beyond that when the sound of his breathing slid momentarily across the uppermost reaches of his consciousness. It was not as labored, or as harsh. Then it was her voice, floating in again.

"After Mendoza died, riding with Diaz, I got a job entertaining in a café near Collegio Militar. It was there I first met Huerta. He taught me to speak English, gave me my first taste of what money can do. Tarant had known Huerta before, and when Rockland sent him down to look into the Delcazar papers, Tarant contacted Huerta to help him. Huerta was there when Tarant came across the portion of the *derrotero* Delcazar's uncle had possessed. That's how Huerta knew Rockland would have it. When Huerta told me about it, I showed him the portion of the map I had—"

Now it was his legs. First it had been his breath, now it was his legs. He realized they were hanging free against the stirrup leathers. He was sitting a horse without tension for the first time since Africano had rolled him. He turned toward Merida. Maybe it was in his face.

"Your legs don't hurt now, do they?"

He was almost afraid to speak. "No," he said, with a strange, husky wonder in his voice. "No."

He had never seen her smile with such rich sincerity, and her voice trembled with a strange, joyful excitation. "Then we can, Crawford, we can!"

He stared at her, unable to answer. Then he averted his head, lips thin against his teeth. Could they? He was afraid to answer it. Yet the pain was gone. He could sit there with the movement of the horse beneath him and its sweaty fetor reaching his nostrils in vagrant waves and feel no pain. And with the cessation of his pain, the other things became more vivid in his consciousness.

He caught the faint honeyed odor of white brush from a draw to his right, and drank in its full sweetness for the first time in months. The woman saw that, and her lips lifted faintly. They reached Rio Diablo and turned northward on its banks. It was the best water between the Nueces and the Rio Grande, yet it was no more than a stream, its mucky course following a sandy bottom that wandered in lazy loops through the *brasada*.

"We're crossing Delcazar's old spread now," Crawford told her. "You can see how much better watering you'd get here than where Rio Diablo turns into Rockland's holdings. That's why Rockland wanted to get hold of this stretch. When Rockland's dad first got the Big O, they say the river was bank full from one end of his pastures to the other. Couple more years and it will be completely dry there."

They passed the borders of what had once belonged to Pio Delcazar and came across a grass-grown pile of stones on a clay bank while it was still dark, a broken, hand-hewn timber thrusting its jagged end skyward from the rubble. Crawford dismounted and moved about the area, bending now and then to squint at certain spots. Then he stared across the river to where another heap of stones stood on the far bank.

"Puenta Piedra," he mused, tugging idly at his scraggly black beard. "I wonder if those stories about a natural stone bridge could have started from one the Spaniards built on the route south from San Antonio."

"How does this line up with Tinaja de la Tortuga?"

He looked upward, turning his head till he found
Lucero, and raised his hand to it. "There's the Shep-
herd's Star. And the one the Mexicans call La Guía.
They're always fixed in relation to each other. That
leaves us almost due south of Turtle Sink."

"That tallies with the map," she said, spreading the
parchment out against her horse's neck. "Red Trails
must be right in the middle of that thicket we skirted.
And this is the Puenta Piedra they mean. We have to
turn east a little now to strike Llano Sacaguista."

He got onto the pinto without hesitation this time,
and led down into the brown muck of the shallow water
and up the other bank. Llano Sacaguista proved to be a
vast open flat covered with greening sacaguista grass.
He had never traversed these particular flats, and beyond
this was a stretch of brush entirely foreign to him. They
left Rio Diablo for a mile or so and then struck it again.
A block in the river caused by some ancient upheaval
rendered the land boggy here. The hollow boom of
bullfrogs mingled with the other night sounds. A 'gator
bellowed somewhere from the depths of the exotic brush.

"Looks more like East Texas," Crawford muttered. "I
wonder if this could be Lost Swamp."

He could see the glow of excitement in the woman's
eyes now. They pushed on southward with the false
dawn dropping an eerie light through the brush, The
boggy section fell behind, and the natural aridity of the
brasada returned. They were still following the river,
though it was nothing but a dry bed now, the trickle of
water having ceased where it ran into Lost Swamp. A
true dawn was bringing light to the sky in the east when
they heard the first sound. It was a thin sibilation, remi-
niscent of the mesquite sighing in a light breeze. Crawford moved his pinto over beside Merida's copperbottom, halting both horses, to sit there, listening. Then
he touched a heel to the pinto's flank, moving it care-

fully down into the very center of the river bed. The brush on either bank grew more dense as they moved on up the dry bed, and began to gather here in the bottoms now. The sound increased, too. The faint hissing was veritably ceaseless now, rising and falling in a sibilant tide. Finally the brush was so thick in the river bed they were having to force their way through. The pinto was beginning to fiddle nervously. It shied, finally, and Crawford jerked it to a stop, a vagrant wave of the old panic gripping him. He sat there a moment, trying to control his breathing.

"You wanted to know where Snake Thickets was," he said. "It looks like we're sitting right on the edge of it."

There was a vague awe in her voice. "It sounds as if all the snakes in Texas had gathered here. Crawford—"

"Don't be loco," he said, seeing it in her eyes. "We wouldn't last two minutes beyond this spot. If those Mexicans cached anything, it sure couldn't have been inside here."

"If?" Her tone was sharp; the excited glow fled her eyes, leaving them narrow and speculative as she looked at him. "You still don't believe there is any money."

"I told you I was skeptical to begin with," said Crawford.

"But the part of the *derrotero* you had—" she moved her hand in a vague, defensive way—"coming all this way, putting up with all that back there—Quartel, Huerta, Whitehead—surely—" She stopped as it must have struck her. A reserve crossed her face, tightening the planes of her cheek, and that speculation deepened in her eyes, accentuating, somehow, the oblique tilt of her brow. "Maybe I was right the first time," she said finally. She leaned toward him slightly. "I guess I should have seen it before this. You're hardly the type, are you? Money wouldn't mean enough to you to put up with that." She stopped again, studying him, and then a faint smile stirred her lips. "Which one of us do you think murdered Otis Rockland?"

He met her eyes for a moment, almost sullenly. Then a vague unrest seeped through him. His saddle creaked as he shifted on the pinto, and he turned his head upward, sniffing. She must have taken it for a discomfort arising from her scrutiny, for that smile on her lips spread perceptibly.

"I didn't think you were that righteous," she said.

He brought his eyes back to hers with an effort, staring a moment before he comprehended. "Look," he said, then, with a careful deliberateness. "I don't give a damn about Rockland being killed. It's me, see. It's purely a selfish motive. I told you. A man gets tired after a while. He gets tired jumping like a jack rabbit every time a tree toad chirps. He gets tired running the brush all day and all night to keep one jump ahead of those badge-packers. He gets tired living on raw meat because he's afraid to build a fire, and sleeping in a bunch of mesquite because he can't get near enough a house to get a blanket, and scratching his face off because he hasn't even got so much as a knife to shave with."

"Then why didn't you leave?"

He opened his mouth to say it. Then he closed it again, staring at her. Finally he shrugged sullenly. "It's my country, that's all."

"Is it?" she said. "Or maybe I'm wrong again. Maybe Quartel was closer to the truth than any of us. Where do you pin the badge? On your undershirt?"

"I didn't think you'd understand," he said.

"It would be the most logical reason for your staying, through all that," she said, studying him. "If you really are hoping·to find Rockland's murderer, that would be the most logical reason."

"Let's close the poke," he said.

"And maybe that about your legs is wrong, too," her

voice probed relentlessly. "That would be a pretty good blind. Who would suspect them of sending in a lawman who couldn't even sit a horse?"

She must have meant it to sting him. He saw some strange satisfaction in her face as he stiffened perceptibly.

"No—Merida—" He held out his hand, losing for a moment all sense of the heavy antipathy which had fallen between them. Then it was that restlessness, coming again, through the consciousness of her mocking eyes on him. The pinto began to fiddle around in the sand, and the woman's copperbottom raised its head, delicate nostrils fluttering. Merida looked at the animals, frowning.

"What is it?" she said.

A puff of wind ruffled Crawford's ducking jacket against his ribs. He turned in the saddle, staring northward. It was light enough with dawn now for him to discern the blackening clouds on the horizon, above the pattern of brush. The breeze whipped through the *brasada* anew, strong enough now to drown out the incessant hissing which emanated from Mogotes Serpientes. Mesquite rattled mournfully to the wind. A mule·deer broke from chaparral with a clatter behind the horses, bounding across the river bed in frightened leaps. The pinto snorted and began fighting the bit, whirling in the sand.

The woman shivered with the sudden chill, calling again, a vague fear tinging her voice. "What is it?"

He could hardly answer. The plunging, rearing pinto had filled him again with that panic, and he was gripping frantically with his legs, blood thickening in his throat, choking him up, sweat breaking out on his face.

"Norther." He finally got it out. "Hits like this sometimes in the spring. Better get to shelter quick as we can. It looks like hell is going to pop its shutters. Delcazar used to have an old jacal on the Diablo. It's south of us somewhere along the bottoms. He and I used to hole up there when we were hunting—"

He was fighting the pinto all the time he shouted, and he could hold it no longer. Frothing at the mouth from battling the bit, the horse wheeled wildly, tossing its head, and bolted up the bank of the river. The wind had risen to a veritable gale already, and the ducking jacket whipped about his torso with a dull slapping sound as the pinto burst through the first growth of chaparral. A hackberry rose ahead. Crawford reined the horse aside desperately, sliding off on one flank to get beneath the branches. He was shaking with panic now, and the pain was in his tense, quivering legs.

"Crawford, Crawford—"

It was Merida's voice behind him. Her animal made a hellish clatter going through a *mogote*. Then that was drowned in the howl of the rising gale. Crawford was dimly aware of his own choked sobbing as he fought to stay on the frenzied pinto and turn it southward toward Delcazar's jacal. His consciousness of the norther was only secondary to the terrible animal panic in him. The black clouds had risen like a pyre of smoke over the northern horizon and were descending on the near brush like an awesome, clutching hand. Already rain was beginning to pelt the thickets. The howling wind tore a pendent bunch of mesquite berries off its bush as Crawford raced by, carrying it into his face. He shouted aloud at it, clawing wildly at the blinding mass. But mostly it was the horse beneath him. The writhing heat of its frenetic movement beating against his legs. The dank smell of its wet body sweeping him. The coarse black hair of its mane whipping into his face. The awful demoralizing consciousness of its uncontrollable run carrying him along.

He could hear his own choked, incoherent cries. The fear held him in a shaking, writhing vise now. Nopal clawed his face. A post-oak branch struck his head with stunning force. He clung to the horse, bawling insanely, no longer trying to rein it, torn off one side by raking chaparral, beaten at by the trunk of a hackberry, scratched and ripped by mesquite.

"Let go, Crawford." It was Merida, calling shrilly from behind him somewhere. "Jump, Crawford, please, let go, oh please—"

"No! no!"

Had he screamed it? Someone was screaming. His head rocked backward to a blow. Sensations spun in a kaleidoscope about him. The towering dominance of a cottonwood reeled around its orbit above him. Mesquite swept into his vision and out again. Sound and sight and feel became a confused pattern. Red-topped nopal swam past. The crash of chaparral dinned in his ears. The gnarled curve of a post oak reeled up and blotted out his vision with a stunning blow in the face. His own hoarse scream of agony. The drum of hoofs somewhere beneath him. The shrieking wind. White brush. Green toboso grass. Brown hackberries. Agony in his legs. The horse whinnying. White brush. Pain. Grass. Screaming. Trees. Shouting. Blood. Nopal—

"Crawford!"

He did not know he had left the horse till he found himself crouched there in a thicket of mesquite, his face against the wet, earthy smell of dampened grama grass, making small, incoherent sounds. He seemed in a void, only dimly aware of sound sweeping around him, his awesome fear the only real thing to him. It clutched his loins and knotted the muscles across his belly. His legs were still rigid and trembling with that pain. He was sobbing in a hoarse, choked way. He heard the creak behind him but didn't know what it was till the woman's voice came through the haze of primal panic.

"Crawford—"

"There. That's it. You've seen it now. All of it. Can we? Hell. How do you like it? Isn't it pretty?"

"You should have jumped." She had dropped to her knees before him and pulled his face up off the ground. The rain had soaked her clothes and when she drew his head into her arms he felt the soft, wet contour of her breast through the damp silk shirt. He was still shaken with that animal fright, and he had no control over his choked, guttural sobbing, or his words.

"I couldn't jump. It's always like that. I'm so scared I want to puke and the only thing I want to do is leave the horse and I can't." His voice sounded muffled against the supple heat of her body. He had never let it out like this before, and with the panic and pain and fear robbing him of all control, he heard all the agony and anguish and frustration of the last months flooding from him in a wild release. He was still crouched on the ground, bent into her lap, his face against her breast, his fingers clutching spasmodically at the grass on either side of her.

She soothed him like a child, stroking his head. Finally, the pain began to die in his legs. The knotted muscles across his belly began to twitch spasmodically, and then relaxed. It was no longer his hoarse, sobbing words against her body. It was only his labored breathing. The full realization of what had happened struck him and he forced his head back in her arms till he was far enough away to see her face. The flush of a sudden shame swept darkly into his cheeks. She saw it, and her eyes widened with a tortured compassion.

"No, Crawford, no, please," she said, in a husky voice, and put her palms against his cheeks and pulled his head to one side. Her position gave weight to the leverage of her hands, and he found himself lying with his back on the ground, with his knees twisted beneath him and Merida bending over from her sitting position.

He had thought about it, before, enough times. A man did, with such a woman. But none of it had equaled this. All the shame was swept away. The sounds of the storm were blotted out. His whole consciousness was of the straining tension of her body against him and the moist resilience of her lips meeting his. Finally she lifted her head, and he could see that her eyes were closed. She sat that way a moment, without opening them, her blouse caught wetly across the curving rise and fall of her breast. He lay staring up at her, and it was not the fear or the pain or the shame any longer in him, or even the passion which had swept him in that brief, violent moment. Opening her eyes, she must have seen it in his twisted, wet face.

"Crawford," she said in a strained voice. "Crawford, what is it? What do you want?"

Chapter Eleven

Old Friends Reunited

THE MEXICANS CONSTRUCTED the roofs of their jacals by laying willow shoots in a herringbone pattern across the bare vigas which formed the rafters, and then piling a foot or so of earth atop the shoots. It was this pattern Crawford saw when he first opened his eyes. Then it was the estufa, built of adobe, in one corner of the room, with a raised hearth and a cone-shaped opening in front, the hood rounding from the center to each wall with two mantels terraced back toward the chimney. It was over this oven that the old man stood.

"Delcazar!"

Crawford's voice turned the aged Mexican, a rusty black frying pan still held in one gnarled fist. His face was seamed like an ancient satchel, and he squinted with the effort of focusing his rheumy eyes on Crawford. His soiled white cotton shirt hung slack from stooped, bony shoulders, and the inevitable *chivarras* were on his skinny legs, glistening with daubs of grease. They gazed at each other in an uncomfortable silence, and finally Delcazar made a vague movement with the frying pan.

"Hard to know what to say," he mumbled. "After such a long time, and all that's happened."

"Yeah." Crawford put the rotting bayeta blanket off him, moving his arms and legs tentatively, grimacing with the pain it caused him. Hail had come after that first downpour of rain, and the white skin of his shoulders was marked with small purple bruises. He sat up, swinging his legs off, watching the Mexican. "I remember we had a terrible time in that storm. Last I recollect is trying to build a fire beneath some coma trees."

"That must have been a long time before I find you,"
said Delcazar. "I was in my jacal here when I hear somebody yelling my name. You was carrying Merida across
your shoulder. Both near froze to death. I put you to
bed like that time in Austin when the red-eye got you."
He saw how Crawford was looking around the dim room,
and Delcazar grinned hesitantly. "She's out getting
water for the coffee."

They were still watching one another that way, waiting, and Crawford waved his hand around the room. "I
didn't think you'd hide out here."

Delcazar bent toward him, squinting. "Hide out?
How do you mean?"

"A lot of people know about it," said Crawford. "I
should think it would be the first place they'd look."

"They?" Then Delcazar seemed to ·understand. He
pointed at himself with a thumb. "You think—that I—
I—" He halted with a confused grunt, staring at Crawford. "Then—you didn't?"

"Don't you know?" said Crawford.

"*Dios,* no," said Delcazar. "How could I know? Bueno
told me how you threaten Rockland after Africano rolled
you. I thought—" he gave a short, rueful laugh—"I guess
I even hoped—"

He trailed off, shrugging hopelessly again, and Crawford bent toward him. "Del, are you trying to tell me
you didn't kill Rockland?"

"Trying!" The old man bristled. "Trying to tell you?
You doubt my—" He broke off, staring at Crawford.
When he spoke again, it was simply, without vehemence.
"No, Crawford. I didn't. I thought you did. You're on
Bible Two. There was a couple of Rangers in the brush.
Torbirio spoke with them. He tell me they had you on
the fugitive list."

His face darkened, and he turned away from Crawford,
setting the frying pan down. From one of the terraced

shelves he took a grease-soaked paper, unwrapping it from about the piece of bacon, rubbing the meat sparingly across the frying pan.

"Isn't that the same piece of side meat you had when we were here last?" said Crawford.

Delcazar tried to smile. "Almost, I guess. Some day I have a hog of my own and we grease the pan with a fresh piece every morning."

"You said you hoped I had killed Rockland," Crawford murmured, watching Delcazar's back. "Why?"

"*Nada*," said Delcazar. "*Nada*."

Crawford's levis had been drying over the fire, and he rose to get them. "Because if I had done it, the whole thing could have been nothing more than the quarrel between me and Rockland?"

The old man pulled a pot of boiled beans out and dumped them into the frying pan. "Frijoles *fritos*, Crawford. You always like them."

"But if it wasn't me who did it," said Crawford, pulling on his damp levis, "there would have to be some other reason for Rockland being murdered. Santa Anna's chests, for instance." He saw Delcazar's whole body stiffen. The beans started to hiss as the flames licked at the bottom of the frying pan. "What do you know, Del?" said Crawford.

"*Nada, nada*." The old man turned around, rising with effort. "I don't know nothing."

"Your uncle was the *capitán* of that mule train," said Crawford.

"My mother tell me that," said Delcazar. "I never seen him. He died in Mexico City when I was a little *niño*."

"Then why are you so het-up if you don't know anything about it?"

"It's dangerous, Crawford," said Delcazar, catching at his arm. "It's the most dangerous thing ever hit this brush. You better get out of it while you're still alive.

It's got the whole *brasada* going now. No telling how many are mixed up in it now. The Mexican government has an agent up here somewhere."

"Huerta?"

"The man at Rockland's?" said Delcazar. "I don't think so."

"Huerta was the one who told me about your uncle," said Crawford. "Funny nobody has come hunting you. You're a logical link."

"They have," said Delcazar. "I wasn't here to greet them."

"Who?"

"That ramrod Tarant hired to clean out the brush," said Delcazar. "Him and his whole *corrida*."

"Quartel?" Crawford's eyes narrowed, staring past Delcazar. "I hadn't thought of him."

"You better think of him. You better think about everybody, Glenn. No telling who's in it, now, and who ain't. No telling who's going to come up behind you next. I hear they take your Henry away—" He turned and squatted by the mess of saddle rigging and blankets in the corner, rummaging around till he came up with a wooden-handled bowie—"Here, it's all I have. I know it seems silly, but you got to have something. I wish I had a gun. That old Remington I owned blew up." He stopped again, clutching Crawford's arm. "Glenn, you ain't going back?"

"Why else did you give me the knife?"

The old man let his hand slide off.

"I guess so. I know you." He sniffled, rubbing peevishly at his coffee-colored nose with a calloused index finger. "I guess there ain't any use trying to keep you from it. They couldn't keep you from it with Whitehead. What are you after there, Glenn?"

Puntales of peeled cedar formed the doorframe. Crawford hefted the bowie in his hand, flipped it into the cedar post with a deft twist of his hand. He walked across the room and pulled it free.

"We found Snake Thickets before the norther hit, Del," he said.

The old man grunted. "You're doing it wrong for a short throw like that. Let me show you."

Crawford had been holding the bowie by the tip of its blade and throwing it from back over his shoulder, allowing it to flip over once in the air before it struck. Delcazar palmed the heavy knife with the hilt against his wrist and the blade on his fingers. He threw it from his hip, point foremost. It struck with a dull thud. Crawford went over to the post. The blade was embedded half an inch deeper than his throws had sent it in. Standing there in the doorway, he turned back to the old man, squinting at him. Delcazar sniffled that way again, rubbing his nose, not meeting Crawford's eyes.

"I told you, Glenn, I never even seen Mogotes Serpientes. If you find it, okay. But I never even seen it. I thought it was just a story, like Resaca Perdida."

"We saw Lost Swamp too," said Crawford. "Snake Thickets was the most interesting, though. You should have heard it. Sounded like those beans, only ten times as much. Must be a million snakes in those *mogotes*." He paced back to Delcazar, palming the knife as the old man had this time, throwing it with a grunt. With the blade quivering in the cedar post, he turned part way to the Mexican. "I guess you know what the woman came from Mexico for. She thinks it's somewhere in Snake Thickets."

Delcazar was shorter than Crawford, and he had to turn his head up to meet the younger man's eyes. "Listen, Glenn," he said soberly, "I don't know what you're in this for. I've heard a lot of reasons. Quartel thinks you got a badge tacked on you somewhere. That might be. A man can get a new job in the time you been away from the

brush. Bueno Bailey said something about trying to clear
yourself of Rockland's murder. That may be, too. If you
didn't kill Rockland, maybe the man who did is at the
Big O spread. Personally, I no care whether you killed
Rockland or not or why you're here. I just no want to
see you messed up in it, that's all. I know you before, and
I no want to see you messed up in it. Take my advice as
an *amigo*. Forget Mogotes Serpientes. Forget the whole
thing. Get out of it. Get out of it right now."

Crawford scratched his beard, squinting into the old
man's eyes thoughtfully. "You know, Del, it just strikes
me. Two men can be friends for a long time, and not
really know each other very well."

"Ah, *carajo*," growled Delcazar, shuffling back to
hunker over the fire.

Crawford watched him stir the steaming beans. "Is
there a way into Snake Thickets, Del?"

"*Nada*," grumbled the old man. "I don't know. I don't
know nothing."

There was a muffled sound from outside, and then
Merida was standing silhouetted in the doorway, staring at Crawford. All his weight lay in his chest and shoulders, and below the line of dark sunburn that covered
his face and neck, the skin was pale and white and so thin
as to gleam almost translucently over the musculature
lying quilted across his upper back. He became aware of
how long Merida had gazed at him like that, without
speaking, and turned farther toward her. The myriad
striations that formed the heavy roll of muscle capping
his shoulders were clearly defined, and the abrupt movement caused a faint ripple beneath the skin, like the stir
of a sleepy snake. Merida smiled strangely as she entered
with a big clay jug of water.

"*Cimarrón*," she said.

"What?" he asked.

"*Cimarrón*," she said. "*Ladino*. I never could quite

think of what you reminded me. Now I know. One of those wild outlaw cattle Quartel brings in from the brush. Sullen, like them. Bitter. Even built like them. Their weight all up in their shoulders, running the brush so constantly they melt the beef off till—"

She stopped short, a strange, indulgent smile catching at her mouth as she saw the puzzled expression in his face. He turned to pull his shirt off the estufa. Merida moved after him, till she stood close behind. Delcazar was across the room, pulling a twist of chili from where he had hung it on a viga. Merida spoke in a low tone that the old man would not hear.

"What was it out there, Glenn?"

"When do you mean?" he said, without turning around.

"You know when I mean," she said. "After I'd kissed you. The way you looked. That expression on your face."

"Nothing," he said stiffly. He couldn't tell her, somehow, if she didn't know. It just wasn't in him to express his own terrible incapacity again, to her. For that was what it had been, out there, after the kiss. The bitter, unutterable realization that no matter how much he wanted her, he was completely unworthy of such a woman, and could never have her.

"It was something," said Merida, tensely, trying to turn him around, "tell me, Crawford, tell me—"

"Hola, Delcazar!" shouted someone, from outside, halting Merida. The old man whirled about, dropping the chili. Quartel had come into view, outside, across the clearing from the doorway, moving into the open from the brush in stiff, tentative steps, his Chihuahuas tinkling softly. He was leading his own *trigueño* and the copper-bottom Merida had ridden. Crawford made an abortive move toward the door, but Delcazar caught him.

"*Buenos dias,*" said Delcazar, stepping then into view.

"I found Merida's horse down in the bottoms," Quartel told him. "I thought they might—ah, the flash rider himself."

He must have seen them behind Delcazar. Crawford pushed past the old man into the open, and saw the morning sunlight catch Quartel's white teeth in that pawky grin. The brush held a torn, rended look after the norther, great holes ripped in the mesquite thicket behind Quartel, mesquite berries littering the ground. The copperbottom shifted wearily, rattling its bridle.

"How did you find us?" said Crawford.

"I trailed you," said Quartel.

"That's some trailing."

Quartel shrugged. "Believe it or not. I don't care. There was someone at the Big O looking for you."

"Yeah?"

"*Si.* I misjudged you, Crawford. Let me apologize for thinking you were a lawman." Merida made a small strained sound from behind Crawford, and Quartel grinned at her. "*Si,* Merida. This man looking for Crawford don't pin it on his undershirt, either. He has it right out where everybody can see. He's hunting Crawford all right. He says he's got orders to shoot him on sight."

Chapter Twelve

CONQUEROR AND CONQUERED

IT WAS TWILIGHT of the same day that Quartel had found them` at Delcazar's jacal. Crawford and Merida had ridden double on the copperbottom back to the Big O, where Merida had gone up to her room to change, while Crawford washed up in the kitchen. No one was in evidence when Crawford returned to the living-room for a drink, feeling exhausted and battered from that night in the storm and the long ride back. He was no connoisseur, his experience with good liquor limited to the few times he had drunk Rockland's potables here, and he was at a loss to choose from the array of glittering bottles and decanters in the sideboard. He sampled one labeled *curaçao* and found it too sweet for his taste. Finally he settled on some armagnac, pouring himself a stiff jolt and moving toward the French windows. He had meant to sit down in one of the willow chairs, but the strange silence outside caught his attention.

It was unnatural for this time of day. There was no wind, and the mesquite berries hung in motionless clusters from drooping trees. Dusk clouded farther thickets, and only the nearest growths took form. The low mats of chaparral crouched like waiting cats in the gloom. The warped dead hackberry by the wagon road thrust skeleton arms skyward. It seemed to be waiting for something too. That oppressive sense of expectancy bore in on Crawford, and he emptied half the glass at one gulp, squinting his eyes as the brandy burned his throat. It did not help. Waiting. The sickish sweet scent of the *lluvia de oro* twining itself through the lattice of the front porch was so oppressive in the hot, still air that it nauseated him. Waiting—

The sound of someone rushing down the stairs caused him to turn toward the door. It was Merida, and he was surprised to see she had not changed from the torn, dirty leggings she had ridden in. Then he saw the expression on her face.

"Where's Quartel?" she cried.

"He went down to the bunkhouse I guess," Crawford told her, frowning. "What is it?"

"He was right."

"Who was right?"

"Quartel," she said, coming across the room in stiff, tense steps, her eyes fixed to his face. "Nexpa saw him."

"Quartel?"

"No," she said. "Crawford, don't you understand? Nexpa saw him from an upstairs bedroom. He's out in the brush and he's coming back."

It struck him, then, whom she meant, and his fingers tightened involuntarily around the glass. "The lawman?" She stared at him without answering, her mouth working faintly. He realized his fingers ached, and he eased his grip on the glass. "That's crazy, Merida. No badge-packer would come in here like that. Even Sheriff Kenmare was afraid to follow me this far. Nexpa must be mistaken." She shook her head, the planes of her face taut and strained-looking, her eyes glued in that wide, frightened way to his. He made a small, frustrated motion with the glass, his voice growing hoarse. "She must be, Merida. No lawman. Not even a Texas Ranger." She shook her head again, emitting a small, sobbing sound. He bent toward her tensely, his chest moving perceptibly with the breath passing through it. He was remembering what Delcazar had said. Bible Two? "It *is* a Ranger?" Crawford almost whispered.

She caught his arm, the words torn from her. "You've got to get out, Crawford. Before he reaches here."

"Ranger," he muttered, almost to himself, turning to get past her toward the door. "It can't be—"

"Too much time, Crawford," she said swiftly, blocking him from that direction. "Can't you understand? He's coming back. You won't even be able to cross the compound before he's here. You won't even be able to reach the brush. You'll never make it on foot, Crawford."

He stared down at her twisted face. "What are you saying?"

"There's one in the small corral," she said. "Nexpa told me. It's one of Jacinto's, so it won't be spooky."

It took him a moment to comprehend what she meant, and then it escaped him in a strangled way. "Think I can do it that way?"

"You've got to." She was close to crying now, the tears glistening in her eyes. "There isn't any other way, Crawford. Can't you understand? You've got to. Right now. You'll never make it to the brush. It's twice as far as the corral. You'd be out there in the open, and you'd be a clay pigeon. Your only chance is the corral."

"No!" He tried to break free of her grip on his arm. "I can't. You know I can't. You saw, out there in the storm, with that pinto."

"You can!" she cried. "You've got to, Crawford, you've got to."

He stared down into her twisted, pale face. Then, with a guttural, inarticulate sound, he whirled to the French windows, opening one farther, and stepped out onto the porch. He stood a moment behind the screen of yellow *lluvia de oro* covering the lattice. The silence lay across the compound so thick it almost gagged him. Waiting. There it was again. His shoulders hunched forward, and his whole tense body had taken on the look of a hunted animal. He stared furtively down the length of the porch. His shirt was wringing wet with sweat now.

"Crawford—"

It came from Merida, standing in the window behind him. Without turning around, he moved down the steps, his boots making a clatter in the silence. Then he was moving across the ground in an urgent, shuffling gait, his narrow, dark head turning ceaselessly from side to side. He realized he was still holding the glass, and threw it from him with a muffled curse. With every step nearer the corral, something seemed to be contracting about his heart. He was fighting for breath, and sweat had turned his beard soggy when he reached the fence. In the semi-gloom, he could barely make out the shape of the horse. This was the corral they broke broncs in, built in three sections, the largest section on this side, with a chute at the other end, and beyond that, a small, tight holding corral not much bigger than a stall, where they held the animals before putting them into the chute to be saddled. It had been Otis Rockland's boast that this smaller section was built so hog-tight and bull-tight it would hold the wildest bronc that ever double-shuffled. The heavy, reinforced cedar bars were so close together a man could not crawl between them but had to go through the gate. This gate itself was built so that it would close automatically, a rawhide rope run from its frame through a pulley on the overhead structure with a bucket of sand hanging at its end. Whenever the gate was open the weight of the sand bucket pulled it closed again, and the drop bar fell automatically into its sockets on the outside.

Crawford stopped at this gate, glancing from one side to another at the brush. There was a small crackle behind the bunkhouse. With a startled abruptness, he pulled the rope that hoisted the drop bar from its sockets and lifted it above the top of the gate, allowing the portal to swing open. The bar would not drop back into position as long as the gate was ajar. Holding the gate open, Crawford found a rock large enough to wedge beneath the bottom bar and keep the sand bucket's weight from pulling the gate closed when he let go. The horse inside snorted softly. Crawford stiffened by the gate post. Then, his whole body so tense the muscles ached, he took a forced, jerky step toward the animal. The horse snorted again, louder. It had been hitched to the corral and, as Crawford drew near, the animal began tugging at the reins nervously.

"Easy, boy, easy." Crawford tried to make his voice soft and reassuring, but it came out tight, harsh. "You're going to break your headstall. Easy, you jughead."

But as he drew near, the horse's efforts to get free became wilder. It whinnied shrilly and reared up. The sound halted Crawford in the middle of the corral, his whole body a rigid line. The reins pulled free of their half hitch on the cedar-post bar, and the animal wheeled away from Crawford toward the far corner of the small corral. Crawford's movements were forced, now, as he moved to catch the animal in that corner. He bent forward slightly to peer at the lines of the beast. The darkness revealed only a hazy impression of broad rump and viciously churning hind legs and a roached mane. The stirrup leathers flapped loosely as the animal moved down the fence, trapped in the corner now by Crawford's advance. He was close to it when the horse wheeled with a strangled, screaming sound and broke toward him in a rush.

"No!"

It escaped Crawford in a hoarse shout. He stood there a moment longer, staring at the horse, his whole face contorted. Then he threw himself to one side, and the animal galloped past. It saw the partly open gate and was in a dead run by the time it reached that side. But in its frantic rush, the beast struck the opening partly broadside, rump crashing against the gate, head slamming into the fence post. The horse reeled back, screaming in rage, and wheeled to go through headfirst. But the blow of its body had jarred loose the rock Crawford had wedged beneath the gate, and the heavy bucket of sand descended with a rush to the ground, slamming the gate shut before the horse reached it. The drop bar outside fell into its sockets with a thud, about the same time the charging horse struck the gate once more. The whole corral shuddered with the impact, but the gate held firm. The dazed horse staggered away from the fence, making thwarted, guttural sounds of pain.

Crawford realized he was trembling now. Pain swept up his legs, and the muscles across his belly began to jump and knot. Still dazed, the horse wheeled about wildly. It caught sight of him again, and all its enraged bestial instincts must have pinned the cause of its pain on Crawford, for the animal screamed once more and rushed him.

"No," shouted Crawford, again, his voice choked with the terrible reasonless fear that inundated him. He whirled and leaped to the high fence, trying to climb it. But he heard the pound of the animal's hoofs behind, and realized he would never make the top in time, and threw himself off. As he rolled to the ground, the animal crashed into the fence where he had been a moment before. Crawford stumbled to his feet, starting in a wild run for the gate which led into the chute. But he saw before he reached it that it was shut tight too. He turned to the other gate, his whole consciousness filled with the sound of the panting, whinnying, snorting animal behind him. At the portal, he tried to reach through and lift the drop bar from its sockets, but the cedar-post log was too heavy. He grabbed the gate, heaving at it madly. The horse was trotting back and forth on the other side of the small corral in a dazed way, shaking its head, snorting. Crouched weakly on his knees by the gate, trembling and shuddering, Crawford tried to keep his voice down, hoping he would not arouse the horse again.

"Jacinto," he called. "I'm in the corral. The bar's

dropped on this gate in the corral and I'm trapped inside with Africano. Jacinto, come and get me out—"

There was no sound from outside. He sagged there, panting, the pain clutching at him spasmodically, clenching his teeth in a desperate battle against the fear.

"Merida! Can't you hear me? Somebody. Jacinto! Come and let me out. The bar's dropped and Africano's in here. That killer's in here and I can't get out. Merida." His voice rose and he began shaking at the gate again. "Someone hear me! Merida! Jacinto! I'm locked in with that black killer—" He was screaming now, throwing himself bodily at the door like a frenzied animal—"Damn you, come and get me out, damn you, Merida, you put that *puro negro* in here, you knew I'd be trapped in here with Africano, someone, come and let me out, for God's sake, Jacinto, let me out, Aforismo, can't you hear me, you can hear me, damn you, oh, God damn you—"

He stopped, huddled against the door, sobbing uncontrollably, realizing his own screams had set the black off again. Crawford jumped away as the horse came at him, stumbling and rolling in the dirt, bawling like a baby, too far gone to realize clearly what he was doing. He tried to claw up the fence again. But that pain in his legs and his terrible fear robbed him of much control. His boots beat a futile tattoo on the bars, seeking the openings in between. His bloody hands clawed blindly for holds. And the fence was too high for him to reach the top before the horse crossed the small corral. Over his shoulder he could see the animal coming.

"No! no! no—"

His wild bellow was cut off as the animal spun broadside against him. He heard his own crushed roar of pain, and he fell off into the dirt, his arms instinctively going over his head to protect them from flailing hoofs as he rolled away. The horse was as wild and frenzied as Crawford now. Two beasts filled the narrow confines of the corral with their crazed screams, forming shadowy, thundering, pounding, running shapes back and forth between the fences, the whole structure shuddering as one or the other smashed into the sides. Crawford did not try again to climb the fence. Hands bloody, clothes covered with dirt, shirt torn, all his wild concentration was on avoiding the mad, blind rushes of the killer horse. He found himself backed up against the door leading into the chute, facing the charging horse. He threw himself bodily aside, and the animal crashed into the door. Panels cracked and splintered, and corral posts groaned with the strain. The *puro negro* stumbled back, blood streaming from its head, eyes showing their whites in the gathering darkness, foam dripping from its jaw.

Crawford had rolled across the short space to the side fence. And crouching there now, watching the horse wheeling and circling, seeking him, a terrible blinding anger swept him, blotting out for a moment the awful fear and pain. They thought they could do this to him? They thought they could lock him in a stall with a killer? The hell—

He dove aside again as the horse rushed, feeling no pain in his legs as he landed, feeling no panic, feeling only that utter rage, scalding, vitriolic, cleansing.

"You think you can do this to me?" he found himself shouting. "Merida? You think you can lock me in here like this? Damn you, Merida!" He moved in front of the door to the chute, yelling crazily at the animal. "Come on, Africano, here I am, you bastard, here I am, come on, see me, damn you, come on—"

Dirt spurted beneath the churning hoofs as the horse charged and reared above the man. Crawford waited till the last moment, jumped aside. Panels cracked and split again as twelve hundred pounds of horseflesh crashed against the gate. The horse staggered off, whirled back to Crawford.

Gasping, Crawford pawed sweat from his eyes, dodged aside. The *puro negro* caught itself before plunging into the fence there, whirling on one hind foot and changing its lead in mid-air to rush Crawford again with a frenzied scream. He put himself in front of the chute door again.

Once more it was the horse's wild scream and the leap aside and the maddened animal shaking the whole corral as it crashed into the door. Another panel cracked, and hinges creaked, and the door sagged outward. Blood covering its head, the black whirled and came at Crawford sideways. It didn't give him enough room on either side, and the black's shoulder caught him as he tried to jump away from the rear fence. He went down, rolling up against the side with a force that stunned him.

The horse had smashed into the rear fence, and it backed away, shaking its head. Sensing Crawford at its side, the animal turned, shifting its weight to kick.

Crawford saw the movement and knew what it meant, and not even hearing his own shout, he clawed up the fence and threw himself directly at the horse's rump. His weight struck the black hocks, and, without leverage, all the kick did was throw him bodily back against the cedar logs. With almost human cunning, Africano jumped forward to clear the space between them so it could catch Crawford with the full force of its kick. He rolled under the hoofs as they lashed out. One of them caught his shoulder and he screamed in agony. Then he was up against the door again.

He didn't know how many more times he drew the black into that door before the portal collapsed. It was all a wild haze of choking dirt and soggy sweat and salty blood and lashing hoofs. Time and time again he waited there at the gate till the last moment, and then jumped free, allowing the horse to batter on into it. And finally, with the whole corral shuddering with the impact, the black crashed through the portal, tearing its lower half clear out and carrying the upper portion of the gate about its head and neck as it stumbled on into the chute. The opposite door to the chute had been left open, and the horse went on through into the larger corral.

Pawing blood and sweat off his face, drawing in a great gulp of air, Crawford staggered out after the animal. It was logical that Merida should have taken this long to hear the racket from the house, but the men from the bunkhouse should have reached the corrals long ago. Jacinto was at the fence with Merida, and Quartel was coming up in his hard-heeled run, followed by Aforismo and the others.

"Crawford," cried Jacinto, "get out between the bars! You can do it now. While Africano's still fighting the door. Are you loco? He's a killer. He'll run you down. You can get away now."

"No," gasped Crawford, "no," and ran on toward the horse where it had dragged the chute door clear out into the middle of the corral. He wasn't finished yet. He knew he had to do it now or never, while the anger still blotted out his fear. He worked the *puro negro* into a corner and got close enough to jerk the shattered door off its neck. The horse tried to break away, but Crawford threw himself in front of it, getting the frenzied, lathered animal back against the fence. One of the hands was belatedly climbing the fence with a rope. Crawford did not wait; he moved in toward the horse.

Screaming like a woman, Africano charged straight at him. There hadn't been enough room between them for the beast to gain much momentum, however. Crawford met it almost head-on, throwing himself partly aside only at the last moment, grabbing the roached mane with one hand and hooking his other arm around beneath the neck and letting the horse's shoulder slam into his hip, **throwing him up and over.**

"Crawford," he heard Jacinto scream, "oh, you fool, Crawford."

He didn't hear any more, then, except the horse's wild, frenzied sounds and the horse's drumming hoofs. He didn't see any more except the black devil beneath him, doing everything within the scope of its vicious cunning to get him off.

It bucked, and he took every jarring drop, screaming triumphantly at the agony it caused him. It rolled, and instead of stepping clear off and waiting till the horse came up again, he rode its belly around, eyes open wide, dodging the death in its flailing legs. There was an insane frustration in the black's eyes as it came onto its feet again and found the man had never left it. The horse rolled again, directing its kicks this time. Still Crawford was on when it came up.

He rolled it from one side of the corral to the other, until it had enough of that, and began going over backward. A man stepping off then would have ultimately lost his touch with the horse too. But Crawford rode its neck when it twisted onto its hips and rode its head when it put its rump into the ground and rode its belly while it was upside down.

The horse rose into a veritable orgasm of mad bucking, pin-wheeling, sunfishing, humping up and coming down with all four feet planted, and knocking most of the consciousness from Crawford every time it landed. Crawford was bleeding at the nose and ears, face covered with blood and sweat, clothes black with dirt. His whole world was one of shocking, jarring pain and a grim, terrible concentration on finishing this.

The horse began rolling again, trying desperately to get the man under its black body, and Crawford went with it, crying openly now, pawing blindly for holds, head rocking as a hoof caught him, lying over the animal's back with his nose streaming blood on its dirty hide.

Finally he felt the animal come to a stop beneath him, legs trembling, barrel heaving, lather dripping off it white as snow. Crawford slumped over, hearing his own sobbing, not knowing whether the wet on his face was sweat or blood or both. He waited for the animal to gather itself again. It didn't. Finally Crawford slid off and his legs collapsed beneath him; he grabbed the horse's cannon bone and pulled himself to his knees, then the mane and pulled himself erect. He bent over and was sick. Choking weakly, he saw them coming from the corral.

"Get away, stay away. I'm taking this horse back in. You wanted him for cow work? You got him." Merida swam into his vision, and he spat out blood and teeth before he could speak again. "And maybe you don't know it, Merida, but you did me a big favor. Yeah. A *big* favor."

Chapter Thirteen

VIOLENCE IN THE BUNKHOUSE

THE MORNING SUN had not yet warmed the mud walls of the bunkshack through, and the dank reek of adobe filled the dog-run as Crawford passed down its narrow corridor toward the kitchen, still limping with the pain of his ride on Africano the evening before. Coming from the run, he almost knocked over Jacinto, who had been sitting propped against the wall on a three-legged stool, his head bent forward on his fat chest.

"What are you doing?" said Crawford.

The huge cook had barely caught himself from falling, and he blinked sleepy eyes up at Crawford in surprise. "Sitting on a stool."

"You been sitting there all night," Crawford accused him.

Jacinto looked sheepishly at the prodigious butcher knife across his lap. "No—I—I just—" He waved the blade suddenly at the room. "Well, why not, you been sleeping up at the big house, and now you come down here, and after all that about Whitehead, and everything else, *sacramento*, how is a man to know what might happen—"

Crawford gazed at him soberly. "*Gracias, amigo,*" he said.

Jacinto grinned in embarrassment, turning to shuffle toward the stove. He put the knife down with a clatter and got the big coffeepot to fill it with water at the butt. When he had it on to boil, he took three clay bowls off a shelf and put them on the table. Seating himself at a bench before the bowls, he spoke again.

"You feel all right this morning?"

Crawford was standing in the doorway, staring emptily toward the house. "No," he said. "Beaten to a pulp."

"I'll fix you some Romero steak," said Jacinto. From the dull red clay bowl he fumbled a grain of corn, carefully picking out the black base with his teeth and spitting it into a second, a blue bowl, dropping the remainder of the kernel into the third, a yellow container. He gave Crawford a sidelong glance. "You told Merida she did you a favor last night. How did you mean?"

"Never mind," said Crawford.

Jacinto plucked another grain from the red bowl, picking out the base with his teeth. "You think she put Africano in there?"

"What else?" said Crawford. "Did *you* see any Rangers around?"

"No," said Jacinto, frowning at him.

"Neither did anybody else," said Crawford. "There weren't any."

Jacinto took out another grain of corn, waving it at Crawford. "You mean you thought you was running from a Ranger?"

Crawford turned away impatiently, pacing toward the door. "That's what she told me."

"*Por supuesto,*" said Jacinto. "Why should Merida do such a thing?"

"Good way to get rid of me as any," said Crawford bitterly.

Jacinto studied him a moment, smiling in a hesitant, puzzled way. Then he tipped the yellow bowl so Crawford could see it was full of pale corn kernels. "Now I have *tortillas* white as the sand in Arroyo Blanco." Grunting, he bent forward to pull the metate nearer his bench, a large oblong block of pumice stone, hollowed out in the upper surface from countless grindings with the pumice rolling pin they called a mano. He poured the hollowed portion full of the corn kernels. "Why should she want to get rid of you?" he said, without looking up.

"I guess she had a good reason," said Crawford.

Jacinto took up the mano, began to grind the corn, the hulls working to the edge of the metate like scum along the edge of a water hole. "That day of the bulltailing, when you and Merida went out into the brush. You found what you wanted?"

"Let's not talk about it," said Crawford.

"And maybe you and her was the only ones who knew where it was, then, no?" said Jacinto. With the edge of his fat hand, he shoved the collection of hulls off into the blue bowl, which contained the black bases he had spit out. "You think that's why she did it?"

Crawford's head jerked from side to side. When he spoke, the frustration was evident in his voice. "How do I know? How do I know anything? Sure we found what we were looking for. You know what it was. Everybody knows. Why do you all keep beating around the thicket this way? Mogotes Serpientes. You know that. Maybe she and I are the only ones who know how to get there. And if I was out of the way, she would be the only one to know. It's what she came up here in the first place for, isn't it? She didn't even try to deny she put that killer horse in there. It's the best reason I can think of."

Jacinto poured a little water into the corn left on the metate, began grinding it again with the mano. "Is it?"

Crawford turned sharply from the door. "What do you mean?"

The paste of corn meal and water Jacinto now had was called masa. He began to pat it into thin *tortillas*. The *comal,* heating over an open fire, was a large plate upon which he cast the *tortillas* to bake, without salt, leavening, or grease.

"I am not too astute in affairs of the heart," said the cook, drawing a heavy breath and wiping sweat off his fat face, "but I have had a few, and have drawn some conclusions about women from them, which I think are as accurate as any conclusions about women can be. They will do strange things when they are in love, Crawford, often cruel things, or brutal. Love to them, when they are enmeshed within it, is all of life, is their whole existence. They will fight for it with their last breath. They will go to any extreme for it. Merida is no ordinary woman. You have seen her fire. You know her depths."

"You're riding a pretty muddy creek," said Crawford.

"I'll clear the water," said Jacinto. "Just give me time. Merida came to you for help, didn't she?"

"You might call it that."

"All right. But she knew you could never be much help in the state you were in. You told me she tried to aid you in conquering it that day you left the bull-tailing."

"So what. Huerta acted like he wanted to help me once too. It was only part of the game he was playing."

"*Lástima de Dios,*" cried Jacinto, clapping fat hands to his brow. "Pity of God. Now I know you must be as loco about Merida as she is about you. Only a man in love could be that blind. Can't you see what she did? That day you and she rode into the *brasada* must have made Merida realize, finally, that the only way you could conquer your fear was to ride Africano again. And she wanted to see you conquer your fear, Crawford. More than anything else. More, even, than finding what she came up here for. More, even, than having you live. She didn't want a half-man. She didn't want a coward. She wanted *you,* the way you used to be, the way she knew you must have been whenever those little flashes of your old self would show themselves."

Crawford had turned around, staring at Jacinto, now. It was beginning to grow in him. The first dim realization of it. An understanding he couldn't name, yet. It prickled the hair on the back of his neck.

"Yes." Jacinto could see the strange wonder in his eyes. "You are beginning to see, no? It took you long enough. There are not many women with that kind of gravel in their craw. Not many women could have done it that way."

It was starting to blossom in Crawford now, a strange, dim exaltation. "Do you realize what it did to me? To come out on the porch that morning and see you standing there beside Whitehead's body, knowing what it meant?" Suddenly he knew how she must have felt. "It doesn't happen to a person often in her life." Suddenly he knew what she had been talking about. "That sort of feeling."

That sort of feeling. He looked around at Jacinto, his eyes wide.

"*Sí*," said Jacinto. "You understand now. It would take a lot of man to accept it, Crawford, even when he understood. It would take *her* kind of man. Admittedly she took a big chance on killing you. Maybe she'd rather have you dead than a coward. That's the kind she is. Not many men could take her. Not many men could realize she sent them out deliberately that way, and still take her."

"Hyacinth," Crawford said almost inaudibly, "Hyacinth—"

"*Sí, sí.*" The gross cook began to chuckle excitedly, for he must have seen what was in Crawford. "You better go to her now, Crawford, before it's too late. She thinks you're through with her, after what you told her last night. She thinks you're not enough of a man to take it that way. But you just didn't understand. Now you do. Go on, Crawford. You won't get a woman with that kind of guts twice in your life. It's almost as good as owning a vinegar roan. I owned a vinegar roan once—"

But Crawford had stopped hearing the cook. It held him completely now. It lifted him so high he didn't feel his feet hit the floor when he started to walk. He moved past Jacinto with a dazed, twisted expression on his face, not even seeing the fat Mexican. The only thing within his awareness was that sweeping, tingling sense of exaltation, so strong and poignant it approached a nausea. The kitchen door faced away from the house, and it was more direct to go through the dog-run and out the bunkhouse; he must have gone that way unconsciously, not remembering his passage through the covered run.

"Where you going?" It penetrated only dully. He kept on walking. Then somebody was in front of him. "I said where you going?"

Innes! The singular odor of sweaty leather reached Crawford from the red-bearded man's buckskin ducking jacket.

"The house," he said, trying to get around the man. Ford Innes shifted again, and this time Crawford was brought up against the man's body. It was like walking into an oak tree.

"Not right now," said Innes.

It was the other things, then, brought in with a clarity almost painful. Bueno Bailey. Sitting at the table. Filing the sear on the trigger of his gun. Aforismo. Sitting on the upper bunk to Crawford's right. His legs dangling over the sideboard.

"Did you ever see the *dichos* on my belduque?" he asked, seriously. "I like the one on this side best. *Tripe is sweet but bowels are better.* Don't you like that one best?"

The contraction of Crawford's muscles began with his calves. They twitched faintly, stiffening up, and the tightening ran up the inside of his legs and pervaded his belly and crossed his chest. His whole body was taut as he took the step back away from contact with Innes.

"That's it," said the red-bearded man.

Bueno's gun was an old 1848 percussion Dragoon, converted to handle cartridges. Rubbing his finger delicately across the sear, Bailey nodded his head approvingly.

"*Bueno,*" he said. "I'll bet the pull isn't more than half a pound on that now."

"Where is Quartel?" asked Crawford.

"If you don't blow your foot off, you'll blow your head off," Innes told Bailey. "I never heard of anybody filing a hair trigger down below a pound."

"Where is Quartel?"

Tongue between his teeth, Bailey slipped the mainspring into the butt of his Dragoon, tightening the strain screw against it carefully. "You don't think that's too much of a hair trigger, do you? I knew a Mexican up in San Antonio that used to carry an old Remington filed down to a quarter-pound pull."

"All right," said Crawford, through his teeth. "I am going up to the house, Innes. Will you get out of my way?"

"That Mex would still be alive if he didn't have the cussed habit of jumping off his horse when it stopped," said Bueno Bailey, slipping the trigger down through the frame and screwing the trigger stud into its proper hole. "But I don't jump off my nag. I get off real easy all the time."

"Please, Innes." It was Jacinto's voice, from behind Crawford. "Let him through this time. It ain't the same as before. Please. It's different. *He's* different. Don't you know? *En el nombre de mi madre.* Can't you see—"

"This *bravo's* pretty good," said Aforismo, swinging his legs. "*Nothing compares with my kiss.* But I guess I like the other *dicho* better. Which do you like best, Crawford?"

"Oh, *Dios.*" Jacinto's voice was quavering now. "Please, Innes. I hate violence so. Let him go. I was not born for such as this. Wassail and song, Innes. Can't we all have wassail and song—"

"*Bueno,*" said Bailey, as he finished tightening the hammer stud and started putting on the metal side plates.

"*Compañeros,* can't you hear me? Wassail and song. No violence. Oh, *carajo*—"

"I'll ask you once more." Crawford's voice was flat. "Get out of my way."

"You're not going any place," said Innes, pulling his buckskin jacket up off the handle of his own gun. "Why don't you sit down?"

"Yeah." Bailey had the walnut grips screwed on. He reached for the barrel, fitting it in place. "Why don't you sit down?"

Crawford stooped over to grab the hilt of Delcazar's bowie in his boot and lunged forward at the same time. He struck Ford Innes doubled over. The red-bearded man expelled his air in a gasp and went down. Crawford let himself go with Innes, rolling off the man as they struck. He came face up with the knife in his hand. It happened so fast that Aforismo only had time to pull his belduque back for the throw. Crawford's position prevented an over-the-shoulder throw such as Aforismo's.

"All right, Del," he grunted, and heaved the bowie from his hip, point foremost, while he was still in the act of rolling off Innes.

"*Chingado!*" he heard Aforismo scream. Bailey's body blocked the view in that same moment. Crawford did not see the blow coming. He shouted hoarsely with the pain of Bueno's Dragoon barrel slashing across his head. Stunned, the most he could do was let his knee fly up. It caught Bailey in the crotch. The man's explosive grunt held a sick agony.

Crawford was still sprawled partly across Innes, the

redheaded man had been striving to free his gun without wasting time trying to get from beneath Crawford.
He had it out now and was twisting to bring it in line.
Blinded by Bailey's blow, Crawford squirmed around,
launching a wild kick at Innes. It caught the redhead's
fist as he pulled the trigger, knocking the gun up. The
Remington's boom filled the room, and the slug knocked
a rain of the whitewash they called *yeso* off the ceiling.

"*Lástima de Dios!*" Aforismo's voice came from somewhere after the shot, "come and pull it out, you *chile,*
come and get it out—"

Crawford struggled to his feet, striving to jerk free of
Bailey. But the man had him about the waist, head
buried against Crawford's belly, hair hanging in greasy
yellow streamers, groaning with the pain of that knee
Crawford had given him in the groin.

Innes still had his Remington. He gripped it with his
left hand too, now, rolling back with the weapon in both
fists to line it up on Crawford. Struggling with Bailey,
Crawford could do only one thing. He threw the weight
of his whole body toward Innes. Bailey tried to jerk him
back, but not soon enough. Before Innes got that Remington turned in the right direction, Crawford was close
enough to lift his leg above the man's face. He saw
Innes's eyes open wide with the realization. Then he felt
flesh and bone crunch beneath his stamping boot.

Lifting his leg robbed Crawford of his balance, and he
fell backward with Bailey's next lunging jerk. They
struck the wall so hard the whole building shook, and
another rain of *yeso* spattered down over them.

"*Cristo,* will somebody take it out? Oh, please, somebody come and take it out—"

Bailey rose up, straddling Crawford. Before the man
could strike, Crawford doubled in beneath him and got
his legs twisted around so he could heave. Bailey went
back with a cry, stumbling into the bench. The plank

splintered beneath his body, and the bench collapsed with him. Innes was getting to his feet, hoarse, desperate sobs rending him. He pawed blindly at his mutilated face with his free hand, blinking his eyes as he tried to find Crawford. He must have caught Crawford's movement against the wall. He whirled that way with the Remington coming up.

Crawford jumped toward him, catching the gun in both hands. Still unable to see, Innes clung desperately to the six-shooter. When Crawford yanked the gun around, it pulled Innes too, swinging him against the wall. Unable to tear the Remington free, Crawford let go with one hand and lurched in close to sink his right fist deep into Innes's square belly.

"That for your three-quarter-pound pull, you *pordiosero,*" shouted somebody from behind Crawford, "that for your bacon grease—"

Innes sagged against the wall with a pitiful sob, still trying to pull the gun against Crawford. Crawford brought that fist in again.

"Oh, *madre, madre,* please come and get it out—"

"That for your hair trigger, you *lépero,* I hope it gives you *corajes,* I hope it gives you worse than fits of the spleen—"

Innes was slumped halfway down the wall now, still making those horrible sobbing sounds as he refused to give up. Crawford shoved the gun clear back against the adobe, and hit him again. The redheaded man slid completely to the floor, dropping the Remington. Crawford whirled around, wondering why Bueno had not come back in. Then he saw who had been yelling.

Bueno Bailey was huddled in a corner, and standing over him, beating at him with the broken end of the bench, was the fat cook. "That for your bacon grease, you *rumbero,*" squealed Jacinto, and the bench made a crunching sound striking Bueno, "that for your—"

Crawford leaped across the room and grabbed the bench before Jacinto could strike again. The huge Mexican fought him crazily, trying to tear loose and get back at Bueno. "Just one more, Crawford, please, just one more. He deserves it. Did you see what they were trying to do with you? *Barba del diablo,* just one more. Look at the scabby *pordiosero—*"

"Who was it didn't like violence?" shouted Crawford.

Jacinto stopped abruptly, looking at Bailey, crouching dazedly against the wall. He stared around at the carnage of the room, the smashed table, Innes sprawled out against the wall clutching his face.

"*A fe mía,*" he said in a hollow voice. "Upon my word. It looks like they turned a *toro* loose." Then his popping eyes came back to Bailey. "I did—that—" he waved an incredulous hand at the man. "No, Crawford, tell me I didn't." Jacinto turned around to clutch at him. "*Violencia. Caramba,* I couldn't, not me, not little Hyacinth of the River. My father would be desecrated. Please, tell me I didn't do it—"

"*Dios,* somebody, come and pull it out, damn you, Crawford, somebody, you *chingados,* come and help me, come and get this *cuchillo,* damn you—"

It was Aforismo's voice, breaking in on Jacinto's plea. Jacinto turned toward the man, where he still sat up in the bunk. Aforismo must still have had his right hand held back over one shoulder to throw his *belduque* when Crawford's knife struck him, for the bowie was up to its hilt through his palm, pinning the hand to the adobe wall. With the inconsistency of a child, the tortured look left Jacinto's sweating face, and he began to chuckle.

"Look at him. Aphorisms? Hah! What good are they now? *Proverbios.* Why don't you give us a saying now, Aforismo?" He had begun to drag the table toward the bunk. "*Dichos?* What right have you got to *dichos?*

Tripe is sweet? Hah! How does that belduque know?"
With a great effort he had managed to climb on the
table and bend over the bunk to grab the hilt of Crawford's bowie. *"Nothing compares with my kiss.* That
makes me laugh. That belduque never kissed anything
but the inside of your belt—"

"*Madre,*" howled Aforismo, "take it easy, will you?"

Jacinto tugged more violently in his effort to pull the
knife from Aforismo's hand. *"Dios,* Crawford, how did
you throw it so hard? No wonder he couldn't get it out.
I'll bet it goes clear through the wall into—Crawford,
where you going?"

He was almost out the door, and he threw it over his
shoulder. "To the house." Crawford ran all the way
across the compound and up the steps and through the
close, suffocating heat of the entrance hall, glancing
through the door of the living-room.

"Merida?" The echo of his voice held a frightening
ring, farther down the hall. "Merida?" he called again,
and whirled to take the stairway up, knocking off a mahogany riser with his boot heel, leaping the whole ellip-
tical landing where the stairway turned, halfway up.
It was recognizable, now, a woman's sobbing, coming
from Merida's bedroom. This door was open, too, and
he stumbled in. Nexpa was crouched at the foot of the
bed with her face in her hands. He grabbed her shoulders, pulling her upward.

"Dónde esta Merida?" he shouted.

The maid turned a face up to him so dark it looked
negroid, her eyes wide and terrified. *"No sabe, no sabe,"*
she gasped.

"What have they done to her?" he cried hoarsely,
shaking Nexpa. "You know. Where is she? Did they
take her? What happened?"

"No sabe," sobbed the maid again. *"Huerta, Huerta—"*

"Huerta took her," shouted Crawford. "What are you

talking about? Where? *Dónde, dónde?"*

"En su cuarto. Merida eo puso alli, en su cuarto!"

"My room?" he said, and dropped her roughly against the footboard and wheeled to run down the hall to the chamber he had occupied, tearing open the door. The reeded mahogany posts supporting the bare tester frame formed a skeleton pattern in the gloom.

"Merida?" he called. He could not see enough in the semidarkness, and he ran to the windows, yanking the heavy overdrapes of dark blue velure away from the window. Noon sunlight flooded the room, turned the damask covering on the wing chair to a gleaming china blue, caught brazenly on the brass fixtures of the Franklin stove in the small fireplace. Then, blinking his eyes, Crawford saw it, and realized what the maid had meant. "In your room. Merida put it there."

On the chintz coverlet of the bed lay his rifle.

Chapter Fourteen

CHALLENGING SNAKE THICKETS

No LONGER DID IT WAIT. No longer did it crouch in passive, latent malignance. Now the evil coma unsheathed its thorns, like a knife-thrower drawing his dirks for the first time. Now the adder-toothed retama struck from beneath the disguise of yellow flowers which had caused the Mexicans to call it flower of gold. Now the deadly Spanish dagger of the devil's head thrust and parried and lunged like a savage fencer.

Ever since Crawford had returned to the Big O, the *brasada* had filled him with a strange, inexplicable sense of biding its time, crouched out there, surrounding them with its sinister, purring, waiting destruction. And now, as if this was what it had anticipated, it seemed to leap forth in all its deadly, ruthless malevolence, like a beast unleashed. Never before had it fought him so, blocking his way impenetrably, cutting and stabbing and striking every foot of the way. And Crawford met its challenge, taking a wild, savage delight in pitting all his skill and strength and experience against the *brasada's* violent, cunning, malicious virulence.

And he had a horse! Knowing it would take something more than an ordinary brush horse to catch Huerta, he had chosen Africano. It had not been broken to the spade bit yet, but would work with a hackamore, and the fact that they had first captured it in the *brasada* indicated a life of running the thickets, which would make it a good brush horse even without training. Just how good, Crawford realized the first thicket they traversed. The *puro negro* met the brush with a fearless, consummate skill, something uncanny about the way it could sense whether the *mogotes* were actually impenetrable or whether they held a weak spot which could be run through. It found holes in thickets Crawford would never have guessed were there, running headlong through the most dense ramaderos without a moment's hesitation. The kind of a horse a brush-popper dreamed about. It was a constant battle, and Crawford fought it with the wild abandon peculiar to the *brasadero* when he was riding the brush like this, shouting at the horse and himself and anything else that wanted to listen, and cursing in two languages at every stabbing, clawing thicket which tried to drag him off.

And the names passed by, as they had before. Silver Persimmons. Turtle Sink. Rio Diablo. Chapotes Platas. He had tried to follow Huerta's trail for a while, but when he had seen the undeviating direction it was taking he had quit tracking and had let the black out. Finally he came crashing through the fringe of chaparral into the clearing above Rio Diablo and swung down off the lathered, heaving horse, and ran toward the jacal. A man was trying to crawl across the threshold of the doorway.

"Crawford," he groaned. "I knew it was you. I heard you coming ten miles off. There never was anybody could match you cussing the brush. I guess that's 'cause there never was anybody loved it the way you do." He tried to rise abruptly, his eyes opening in a glazed way as he stared past Crawford. "*Dios,* Africano!"

Crawford had reached him by then. "What happened, Del? They did this to you?"

Dried blood darkened the old man's face, and the soles of his bare feet had a red, blistered look. "You got a hackamore on it," said Delcazar vacantly, still staring at the black. "You can't ride that killer with a hackamore. You're loco—"

"Who did it? Tell me who did it!" almost shouted

Crawford.

"Merida—"

"She did this!"

"No, no," gasped Delcazar weakly. "Merida come first. She say she needed help. Say you weren't with her any more for some reason. Had an idea I knew about Snake Thickets. While she was still here, Huerta came. Followed her, I guess. He thought I knew about Snake Thickets too. Those cigarettes of Huerta's. I'm a *viejo,* an old man. I couldn't stand much. The woman try to stop him. She couldn't do it."

"How do you get. in, Delcazar?" Crawford's voice shook with its low intensity.

Delcazar's eyes widened. "Crawford, you ain't going to try and follow them. It's suicide. Even if you know how to get in. Those *serpientes.* You been there. You heard them. Please, you and I been *amigos* too long. Let those fools kill themselves after a chest of pesos. Who wants pesos—"

"How do you get in?"

Crawford's voice held a shrill, driven stridor that stiffened Delcazar. The old man stared at him a moment, mouth open slightly. Maybe it was the pale, set look to Crawford's face.

"Rio Diablo. You know how it goes underground about a mile above here. Nobody's ever been able to find where it comes up again. It comes from the Nueces past here and then drops out of sight and there ain't nothing left but the dry bed going on south to Mogotes Serpientes. I'll tell you where it does come up again. Right inside Snake Thickets. That's why nobody ever found it. You know how water in a place like Turtle Sink dries up during the day. Then, come night, it rises to the surface again. That's what happens inside Mogotes Serpientes. During the day, the part of Rio Diablo that surfaces inside the thickets is all dried up. Then when evening sets in, it comes up again. That's how you get in. You got to run a short stretch of the thicket before you reach water. That's why you have to time it right. The snakes sleep during the day, and start to stir around at sundown. That's about the same time the water starts rising. If you start in just a few minutes before the sun sets, you can run that stretch of thicket between the outside and the water while the snakes are still asleep. Naturally you'll wake them, but you got a bigger chance of reaching the water than if they were already wide-awake and waiting for you. Once you're in the bog, you're safe. The snakes will come down to drink, but rattlers like dry land too much to go swimming in that muck. Time it wrong by one minute either way and you're done. If you go in too early and the water ain't risen yet, you're setting right in the middle of a million rattlers. And if you go in too late and the snakes are stirring around, they'll probably get you before you reach water. I found it out from an old Comanche a long time ago, Crawford. I was afraid to tell. I was afraid to go in myself and I was afraid somebody would make me show them the way if I tell, and I couldn't do that, Crawford, nobody could. It's suicide. Maybe those Mexicans do it once, with the chests. It couldn't be done again in a million years."

"Still got those cavalry boots?"

"Crawford, please, you ain't going to—"

"I'll want your batwings too."

Delcazar began to cry without sound, and the words came between his lips with a resigned audibility. "In the jacal. Under my bunk."

Crawford stepped past the man, the decision hard and crystallized in him now, permitting no other considerations. He hauled out the old pair of jack boots someone in Delcazar's family had worn with Diaz, and unhooked a tattered pair of batwing chaps from the bunk post, a rarity in this border section where most men preferred *chivarras*. He pulled the ancient Chimayo from the bunk and began cutting it in strips with the bowie. Then he wound the strips about his legs like puttees, up to his crotch, till they formed three or four layers; he had trouble pulling the jack boots on over this thickness.

"*Pechero?*" he said, swiftly buckling the bull-hide chaps on.

Delcazar was huddled against the doorframe, watching him hopelessly. "Had one somewhere. Maybe under the bunk too."

The *pechero* was a buckskin shield used by the *brasaderos* for popping the heaviest brush; it fitted around the front of the horse's chest, tying over its withers and behind its front legs. The black was too weary for any objection as Crawford lashed the *pechero* on.

"Gloves," Delcazar was motioning vaguely toward the fireplace, "gloves—"

They were on one of the shelves above the estufa, thick buckskin gloves with flaps as long as the forearm. Crawford pulled them on his hands and stepped past the old man. He stopped there a moment, staring down at Delcazar. His mouth twisted open as if he would speak. No words came. A torn look crossed his face momentarily. Then he turned and swung aboard the black and jerked the hackamore against its neck and the animal wheeled and broke into a gallop down toward the brush lining the river—

The sun was low and he forced the flagging *puro negro* down Rio Diablo until the water ceased and they were running the dry bed. The mesquite became thicker in the bottom lands, interspersed by cottonwoods turning sear with the heat of oncoming summer. Finally the *pechero* was rattling and scraping constantly against the brush as Crawford forced his way through. He

was riding at a walk now, head cocked to listen, eyes rov-
ing the terrain restlessly, whole body tense with waiting
for the first sign that he had reached Mogotes Serpientes.
The sun was almost down now, and he was filled with
a growing, trembling sense of urgency. Maybe it was the
incessant clash of brush against the buckskin shield
which hid the other sound at first. Suddenly he pulled
the black to a halt. It came from ahead of him, a faint,
barely perceptible hissing sound. He sat there a moment,
letting the thought of Merida in there harden the resolve
within himself till it was so sharp and clear it hurt. The
black had begun fretting at the sound, and Crawford
pulled in the *mecate* on the hackamore, bending forward.

"All right," he said, "we're going through!"

Perhaps it was the tone of his voice. The horse ceased
all movement abruptly, stiffening beneath him. Then the
man flapped his legs out wide and brought his spurs in
against the sweating black flanks with a hoarse shout.
The *puro negro* leaped forward like a startled buck,
breaking into a headlong gallop straight into the brush
thickening in the river bottom ahead of them. Crawford
rode as if he were bareback, gripping the animal from
his thighs down, heels turned in hard against the horse.
They crashed headlong through the first thicket of mesquite, Crawford bent forward with his free arm thrown
in front of his face, the branches ripping at his cheeks
and tearing his levi ducking jacket half off his back. A
post oak loomed before them as they tore free of the
mesquite. He reined the black viciously to one side and
the animal reacted with a violence that would have un-
seated Crawford but for that grip of his legs, wheeling
so sharply the man's torso was snapped to one side like
the flirt of a rope. Crawford jerked himself back in time
to bend down off one side as they passed beneath the
branches. Then they were racing at a thicket of chapar-

ral and huisache entwined together so thickly it formed a solid mat before them. Crawford felt the confidence of the horse beneath him and gave the animal its head, and they crashed headlong through the hole Africano had spotted with his uncanny instinct. Filled with the wild excitement of it, Crawford had begun shouting and swearing that way again, adding his own hoarse obscenities to the roar of popping brush. But even all this sound did not obliterate the noise. It came through his bellow and the crash of brush with an insidious, sinister insistence, that constant menacing hiss, like the threat of escaping steam. It filled him with an excitation which did not come from the mad ride. And as he burst through the chaparral into the open, the first snake struck.

It happened so fast his own reaction did not come till the snake had gone again. He had a dim sense of a sudden writhing shape leaping from the last of the chaparral they were coming out of, and the sharp snapping thud somewhere in front of him, and the horse's leap sideways, screaming. Again his terrible grip was the only thing that kept the man in the saddle, and they were tearing forward once more with a vague impression of that writhing shape slithering off into the brush. They were crashing into the next *mogote* before Crawford realized the snake must have struck that *pechero* on the horse's chest. Now more of them were in sight. Fast as he was going, he could still see the sleepy torpidity of the awakening snakes. He spotted what he thought was a root lying in the thickness of a *mogote,* but as the black jumped it, the root came alive, jerking in a surprised, sluggish way, and then one end began to curl inward. But by the time the serpent had awakened fully and snapped into its coil, Africano was by.

Another one ahead woke faster. Crawford did not see it till a flashing motion filled the lower corner of his vision. Again he heard the sharp thump of the snake striking that *pechero,* and saw the frustrated serpent drop away from the shield in a stunned way. The horse was in a veritable frenzy now, lather foaming its mouth, screaming and whinnying and fighting the hackamore madly without actually trying to change its direction. It was no longer only the hissing all about them. It was the movement. On every side the thickets seemed to have come alive. Writhing, slithering shapes undulating in dim spasms through the pattern of brush. But the fact that they were still awakening and the speed at which Crawford was going aborted the greater part of their efforts. Time and again he saw a snake strike after he was already by. Twice more one of them reached the horse, only to batter its head against that stiff shield of cowhide. Then, beneath him, Crawford heard a thick, slopping sound, and the black stumbled, and almost went down. With his spurs he forced the animal farther on into the muck. It was not very deep and there were patches of dry ground, but there was no more of that nightmarish movement about him now. Only the incessant sinister sibilation to his rear.

His body was drenched with perspiration, and for the first time he realized he was panting in a choked, rasping way. The horse was heaving beneath him, still fighting the hackamore and fiddling around wildly. He suddenly felt as if he were going to collapse. He bent forward, gripping the saddle horn, realizing it was only reaction. Then, as strength returned in slow, undulating waves, the black stopped abruptly, head raised, ears stiffened. Crawford automatically put his heels into the animal. The *puro negro* stood adamant. Then Crawford heard it, and stopped trying to force Africano ahead. Suddenly the horse threw up its head and let out a shrill, wild whinny.

"Damn you," snarled Crawford in a guttural voice. "I ought to—"

He stopped at the answering whinny from farther in the brush. "Crawford?" asked someone from there.

Crawford felt his body straighten involuntarily in the saddle. "Yes, Quartel," he said.

Chapter Fifteen

TREASURE HUNT CLIMAX

PERHAPS IT WAS THE SOUND. The constant, incessant, unrelenting sound of those snakes. Standing in this narrow strip of bog formed by the rising muck of the underground river, the hissing was audible on both sides now. There was something infinitely evil about it that clutched at a man's vitals. It filled Crawford with a vague, primal panic, akin to the fear he had known of Africano before, yet different, in a subtle, insidious way.

"I knew it was you." Quartel's voice startled him, coming from an entirely different direction than before. "I heard you coming. I wish I could cuss the way you can, Crawford." It was getting on Crawford's nerves. The black was becoming unmanageable beneath him. Under other circumstances he would have been willing to play the game. But the thought of Merida somewhere in there drove all the conditioned wariness from him. Suddenly the black raised its head again; he pulled on the hackamore to stifle the whinny in its throat, but he saw which direction it was turned in. He flapped his legs out wide and brought the heels in hard, bolting the black into the mesquite. They crashed through the *mogote*. Crawford had the Henry in his right hand as they burst into the open, keeping it free of brush with the lever down. A vague, blurred impression of Quartel sitting that *trigueño* leaped into Crawford's vision. With one motion he was jerking the hackamore against the left side of the black's neck to wheel it toward the man, and then releasing the hackamore completely to have both hands for his rifle, bringing the Henry up into line with his right hand and slapping his left palm against the barrel at the same time. In that last instant, as fast as he had moved, he had time to see why Quartel had been doing it this way. The man had no gun in his hand. Even as Crawford wheeled and brought his Henry up, Quartel was leaning forward with a grunt, his arm snapping out.

Crawford tried to duck the rope and fire at the same time. He heard his bullet clatter through brush, after the thunder of the shot, and knew he had missed. Then the edge of the loop struck his hand and slid down his arm and closed over the gun. It was either let go the Henry or be jerked from his horse.

The rifle bounced along the ground, and for a moment it looked as if Quartel were going to be able to pull it to him. Then it slipped from the noose. The Mexican wheeled his *trigueño* toward the rifle, and his intent was patent. Crawford turned the black and quartered in on a line that would bring him between Quartel and the Henry. Seeing how he would be blocked off from reaching the gun, Quartel reared his horse to a stop, flirting in his rope and catching it up in loops. Crawford, realizing that if he turned to approach the Henry his back would be to Quartel and the man would have him with that rope, halted his black too. For a moment, the two men sat there facing each other across the open ground. It must have struck Quartel how it had to be, now, about the same time the realization came to Crawford. The Mexican let out a hoarse, violent laugh.

"All right," he said. "I am the best roper in the world, Crawford."

He sat there, grinning, allowing Crawford to unlash the 40-foot rawhide lasso from the black's rig. A picture formed in Crawford's mind that filled him with a growing tension. A picture of Quartel blindfolded on that *trigueño* in the corral with one end of a rawhide dally tied about his neck and ten snorting, stamping, vicious *ladinos* tearing up the turf and the strange sighing sound rising from the crowd of sweating, stinking *vaqueros* every time he threw the bull. It didn't help a man. It didn't help a man while he unhitched the rawhide lashing on the saddle skirt from about the dally and shook out the loops and watched the braided hondo slide down the slick rope. His motions were stiff, jerky. He hadn't roped in a long time.

"Hola!" bellowed Quartel, and those great Chihuahua spurs rolled down the flanks of his brown animal like cart wheels digging ruts in a road. Crawford jabbed his own guthooks into the black, and Africano jumped into a dead run. The brown horse seemed to come at Crawford in a surge that left no space for conscious thought. He knew what a mistake it would be for him to make the first pass, and he bent forward in the saddle, watching Quartel's hand.

But the Mexican was waiting too, and the *trigueño* was completely past Crawford, with Crawford still holding his rope and twisting around so he could watch Quartel, when the man made his throw. The Mexican passed the rope over his shoulder, without looking at Crawford. In that position, the movement of Quartel's arms was blocked off by his body, and Crawford did not know the Mexican had made his toss till he saw the small, tight loop spinning directly over his head. The throw was calculated to compensate for Crawford's forward speed. All he could do to escape it was rein to one side or the other. He bent forward so far on Africano his chest struck the saddle horn, putting the reins against the black neck hard.

The violence of the quarter turn almost snapped Crawford from the saddle. He shouted with the pain stabbing through his middle. He heard the faint sound of the rope striking Africano's rump. Then he was tearing into a *mogote* of mesquite.

Instead of going on through, he wheeled Africano

within the thicket. The horse reared up, screaming with the pain of turning in that cruel brush, and Crawford was charging out the way he had come.

Evidently expecting Crawford to go on through the mesquite, Quartel was racing around the fringe to intercept him on the other side. This caused the Mexican to be at Crawford's rear as he burst out the same spot he had gone in. Crawford put his reins against Africano's neck, and again the horse responded with that incredible turn, and Crawford found himself directly behind the churning brown rump of the *trigueño*. The Mexican was already in the act of wheeling his horse around to meet Crawford. Then he must have seen how Crawford had turned after him, and realized how his own maneuver would place him, for he tried to turn back. It was too late.

Quartel's first turn had placed him broadside to Crawford's oncoming black. Crawford had that one free pass at Quartel's flank, with the Mexican in no position to defend himself by a throw of his own. Crawford saw his loop settle over the man's head.

"All right," he shouted, and dallied his end of the rope around the saddle horn, wheeling Africano away to pull Quartel off.

But there was no weight on the rope. It fell slackly from the horn, and Crawford twisted back to see what had happened.

He had seen Indians do it. One instant Quartel had been sitting the horse, the next he wasn't. The loop fell across the back of the riderless *trigueño*, caught on the cantle, slipped off. Then the Mexican appeared in the saddle again. He had jumped completely off, hanging onto the horn with but one hand, to strike the ground and bounce back up, the rope hitting while he was off on the far side that way.

The first wild action had left no time for much thought, but now, as he recovered his rope and maneuvered to meet Quartel's next move, the sheer dead-liness of this struck Crawford fully. Like trying to figure out three or four plays ahead in a poker game, with your life in the pot instead of a few dollars. Well, he had been figuring one play ahead, ever since he had seen the cards Quartel put down back there at the bull-tailing. It was the trick Quartel had used on Indita. Crawford had spotted the weakness of it, even then. A man could take advantage of that, if he had a horse which could turn quick enough.

Crawford remembered Quartel and Indita had been racing head-on at each other, and he placed himself in the position to meet Quartel that way as the Mexican trotted toward him from across the clearing now. The *trigueño* was picking up its feet in a high, excited action, lather marbling its snout and chest.

"*Vamanos*," Quartel roared, and raked the animal's bloody flanks with his Chihuahua can openers, and they were racing at each other again. Quartel leaned forward and threw his arm out with a grunt as they went by one another. Crawford's own arm stiffened with the impulse to make his throw. Then he realized Quartel's clothesline was not coming.

The rest of it moved automatically, without any conscious volition from Crawford. Holding his throw, he allowed the black to race on past Quartel. Then, when he knew Quartel would be wheeling that *trigueño* to make his true cast at Crawford's retreating back, Craw-ford yanked the *mecate* against Africano's neck. He felt the movement of the horse's shoulders beneath him, changing leads as it spun in full gallop on its hind foot. No quarter turn this time. A half turn, switching ends completely in that instant, so that he was facing Quartel instead of going away and, with the horse still in motion, was racing back toward the Mexican.

It caused Quartel's rope to overshoot completely.

Crawford saw the man's face twist in surprise. Then Crawford made his cast. It was an underhanded throw with a hooley-ann at the end. In wheeling, Quartel had come to a full stop. He made one last abortive effort to turn his animal away, but the small loop caught him before the *trigueño* reacted. Then Crawford was on past the Mexican, with the rope dallied on his horn and snapping taut. He heard Quartel make a strangled sound of pain. Then there was the thump of him striking the ground.

Crawford tried to keep his black in full gallop and drag Quartel, but something within him rebelled. He halted the animal and swung off, running back to catch the man before he could rise. Quartel was on his knees, that rope still about his thick neck, shaking his head dully. The mesquite rattled behind Quartel, and Merida stepped out. She must have passed the Henry where it had been dropped. She held it cocked in both hands, and her bosom was heaving, her face torn and bleeding from the brush she had run through. They stared at each other without speaking. Her eyes were wide and shining, and her lips started twisting across her teeth without any sound coming out.

Then, without any consciousness of having moved, he found her body in his arms and her lips against his and the sound of her expelled breath hot and hoarse in his ears. He didn't know how long he was lost in it. Finally the other things began to come. The cold, hard feel of the rifle barrel against his back where she held it in one hand with that arm around him. The guttural sounds of pain Quartel was making trying to get that noose off his neck. The crash of another passage through the mesquite.

"Crawford, Crawford, I knew you'd come, I knew they couldn't stop you, none of them—" It was Merida, whispering it in a husky, passionate, barely coherent stream against his chest. "I was so afraid. Thinking of you out there. All those snakes. I wanted you to come and I didn't want you to. I didn't know what I wanted. I do now, I mean. I guess I haven't known really what I wanted all my life, but I do now. I was so afraid—"

"Merida— Where are you?"

It was Huerta's voice, accompanying the rattle of the thicket. Crawford lifted his face from the woman's, staring at the doctor as he stumbled from the mesquite. The man's fustian was ripped and torn, and he was dabbing at a cut on his cheek with a silk monogrammed handkerchief. He brought himself to an abrupt halt, breathing heavily, when he saw them.

Crawford disengaged himself from Merida, taking the rifle out of her hand, still looking at the doctor. There was something about the man that vaguely puzzled him.

"Did you find it?" Crawford asked Merida finally.

A dim, bitter expression entered Merida's face. "Yes," she said, "we found it."

"What do you mean?" Crawford muttered.

She inclined her head through the mesquite, that strange expression still on her features. Crawford frowned at her. Then he turned to jerk the Henry at Quartel. The man had finally got that rope off his neck and stood there rubbing the bruised flesh sullenly. He moved ahead of Crawford through the brush.

"You too, Doctor," said Crawford.

They passed through the thicket and crossed a boggy section. With the violence of the action over now, the hissing of the snakes began to impinge on Crawford's consciousness again. Rising out of the bog to the thick mat of greenish-brown toboso grass covering an island of firm ground, they reached the first aparejo. It was one of the old X-shaped packsaddles used by the original Mexican muleteers, with two brass-bound chests lashed into it so that one would fall on each side of the mule.

"The Mexicans carrying this stuff must have been following the dry river bed and hit the fringe of Snake Thickets about dusk," said Merida. "That's the only way they could have got this far in. Then, when the snakes started waking up, and they realized what they had wandered into, the men left the stuff here, knowing it would be as safe as anywhere they could have hidden it, and shot their way out through the snakes again."

"Did you just stumble onto it too?" Crawford asked.

"Quartel had the other third of the *derrotero*," said Merida.

"Quartel?" Crawford's head lifted sharply to the man. He emitted a small, humorless laugh. "That explains a lot of things."

"Does it?" said Quartel.

"It showed Quartel how to find the aparejos once he was inside Mogotes Serpientes," Merida said. "But not how to find Snake Thickets." Her eyes were on Crawford, and that odd expression still filled her face. She moved her head toward the chest. "Go ahead," she said.

He kept Quartel and Huerta in sight when he knelt. The wood was rotten and someone had torn the lid of one chest away from its brass bindings. He lifted it, and stared at the black gunpowder filling the oak box. The woman's voice sounded far away.

"The Centralists must have done this. They would have done anything to break Santa Anna's power at that time. They knew his men were ready to desert because they hadn't been paid in three months. It was only by the promise of this pay that Santa Anna held them together long enough to fight the battle of San Jacinto. You can imagine their reaction if the train had reached the army and they had found their pay to be nothing more than this." She stared emptily at the case. "Twenty chests of gunpowder. That's ironic, isn't it? All this trouble over twenty chests of gunpowder."

Crawford rose slowly, drawing himself back to present necessities by a distinct effort. "We'd better start thinking about getting out of here."

Huerta's feet made a small, quick shift against the toboso grass. Crawford realized what it was in the man now. That air of infinite ennui was beginning to dissipate before something else; an indefinable tension tightened the little muscles about Huerta's mouth till the soft flesh was furrowed like an old man's. The bluish, veined lower lid of his right eye was twitching noticeably. "We can't go out now," he said, and the strain was palpable in his voice. "Not through all those snakes again. They're awake now."

"This place dries up come daylight," said Crawford. "It won't be any safer than out there. We have to leave sometime before then, and it might as well be now."

He began peeling off his gloves and handing them to Merida; then his heavy denim ducking jacket and the bull-hide chaps. Huerta's breathing became more audible as he watched it.

"No," he said, "no—listen—"

"What's wrong with your gun?" Crawford asked Quartel.

"Merida's horse got hit by a snake about halfway through," said the Mexican. "She got pitched and Huerta wouldn't stop to pick her up. I was following them pretty close and came across her before she'd been caught by the snakes. But they were all waked up in that section and I used my lead up shooting our way on into here. That's why I had to use the rope on you."

"What caliber you got?"

Quartel looked surprised. "It's an old Bisley .44."

From the pocket of his levis, Crawford pulled a handful of his .44 flat-noses. He stood there with the copper cartridges in his hand, meeting Quartel's eyes. He held out his hand.

Quartel stared at the handful of shells, then he threw back his head and let out that Gargantuan laugh. "Crawford, you're the craziest *barrachon* I ever saw."

He took the cartridges and broke his Bisley and began thumbing them into the cylinder. Huerta lowered the handkerchief from his scratched face, and his effort at control was more obvious now.

"I haven't got a gun," he said.

"That's too bad," said Crawford.

"No, no, listen, you can't expect me to go out there without—"

He turned around and indicated Quartel should follow him through the mesquite to their horses. Like the well-trained roper it was, the *trigueño* had stopped the instant Quartel left its back, and was standing in the same spot they had left it. Africano must have run on across the bog and been stopped by his fear of the snakes in the first dry thickets over there, for he came trotting back through the mud, whinnying nervously. Crawford blocked the animal off against a *mogote* of chaparral and caught it.

"Get on first," he told the girl.

"Crawford," Huerta began again, "you can't—"

"Get your horse if you're coming with us," he told the man.

Huerta opened his mouth to say something more; then, with a strangled, inarticulate sound, he turned and crashed back through the mesquite. In a moment he returned on the copperbottom. It was a risky thing to do with such a green horse, but there was no other way, and Crawford swung onto the black behind the cantle. The animal kicked in a startled, angry way and started to buck. Crawford swung his arms around in front of Merida to grab the *mecate* and yank back hard on it, spurring Africano at the same time. The *puro negro* quit bucking and broke forward, slopping into a muddy stretch. Crawford turned the horse to get Quartel in front of him. They rode toward the edge of the bog that way.

"You go first, Quartel," Crawford said. "I'll follow you, Huerta. If you can keep your head and stay in between us, we might be able to get you out. Just keep your head. That's the whole thing. Get panicky and you're through. You can even get bit a couple of times by snakes and still live to tell about it if you don't let it throw you. It isn't the venom that kills a man so quick; it's when he gets spooked and starts running and yelling and pumping all that poison through him a hundred times as fast as it would spread if he just stayed calm. Savvy?"

Huerta's copperbottom fiddled beneath him. "Crawford, I can't. Not without a gun. You can't ask me to."

"Quartel?" said Crawford.

"*Si,*" grinned the Mexican, and flapped his feet out wide. The *trigueño* bolted before Quartel's feet came back in to kick his flanks, and then crashed into the thickets. Crawford held the Henry in one hand and he waved it at Huerta.

"Get going, damn you, I'm not going to wait for you to puke, get going!"

"No, I can't, not through there—" Huerta saw Crawford swing out his feet, and whirled the copperbottom with a last desperate shout, and crashed into the Snake Thickets after Quartel. Then Crawford's heels struck the black, and they were going.

At first it was only the wild, crashing, pounding, yelling run through the mesquite. With Quartel leading the way all they had to do was follow the trail he made, running through holes he had burst in the thickets ahead of them. Then the snakes began. First it was that sharp, dry thump against Africano's *pechero,* and the woman's shrill, startled cry. Quartel's gun crashed from ahead of them, but Crawford was too taken up with reining the black to use his Henry. He had that blurred impression of violent undulation around him. There was another snapping thud against Africano's buckskin shield, and a big diamondback fell to the ground beneath them as they went by.

Then it was the shrill scream from Huerta's copper-bottom ahead. Crawford saw the huge rattler dropping off the animal's rump, and the copperbottom started to buck.

"There it is," screamed Huerta, "there it is!"

"Don't lose your head," shouted Crawford. "Get him to running again. He'll last through, Huerta, get him to running—"

Another rattler flashed from the thickets. The copper-bottom reared up as the snake struck, pawing the air wildly. Crawford came up from behind at a dead run and Huerta's panicky reining brought the copperbottom down broadside to them. Crawford jerked his whole body to the left with the desperation of his attempt to rein the black around, but Africano smashed head-on into Huerta's animal.

Crawford had the sense of falling through a bedlam of Huerta's wild yells and Merida's voice calling something and the animal's frenzied, agonized screaming. Then he hit the ground with Merida coming down on top of him. It knocked the breath from him and he struggled to get from beneath her, making a horrible retching sound in his fight for breath. He got to his knees, surprised that he still clutched the Henry. The copperbottom was al-ready crashing off through the brush, and Africano was just scrambling to his feet. Crawford lurched at the black horse, but Africano whirled and galloped at a *ramadero* of *cejas*, smashing through and disappearing. There was a whirring sound from behind and Merida's shriek. He whirled, snapping the lever on his Henry down at the same time, and fired from the hip at the serpent coiled just beyond her. She had been in the act of throwing herself away, and the slug driving into the snake aborted its strike. The head fell heavily to the ground with only half its length uncoiled. Crawford leaped to Merida, grabbing her roughly by the elbow and yanking her erect.

"Crawford, get me out, Crawford! Crawford!" It was Huerta, rising from the patch of switch mesquite where he had been thrown. There was a sallow, putty color to his face and that eye was twitching uncontrollably now. He staggered toward them, his blasé, jaded sophistication swept away before the terrible animal fear. A deadly rattle rose from behind him and he tried to run, and stumbled, falling against Crawford.

The woman's gasp made Crawford turn in the direction she was looking, and he brought up the Henry, kicking free of Huerta, firing at the snake which had writhed from the switch mesquite toward them, shouting at Huerta. "Get up, then. I'll get you out. Get up!"

Panting, sobbing hoarsely, Huerta pulled himself up, staring about him wildly, starting like a frightened deer at every new sound. Crawford put the woman directly before him and started moving forward. Huerta cringed at his side, clawing at him, and he had to keep shoving the man away.

"Hurry, Crawford, hurry, please, what are you doing this for? We'll never—"

"Let go," Crawford bawled at him. "It won't do to lose our heads and start running. How can I—"

"No, Crawford, no—"

Shouting it, Huerta reeled back against him. Crawford had to fight the man off and wheel that way and fire all at once. He couldn't have hit the snake anyway. It had already been in the middle of its lunge.

"I'm hit," screamed Huerta. "Crawford, I'm hit. Save me. I'll do anything. Help me!"

"Keep your head, Huerta. Quit fighting like that!"

"No, Crawford, for God's sake!" Huerta was floundering around blindly, shouting and clutching at Crawford, who tried to kick him away so he could keep the gun going. Another rattler slithered from the thickets, and he fired wildly at it.

"Huerta!" cried Merida, tearing at the man, the panic gripping her voice and twisting her face, "don't be a fool. Let him go, let him go—"

"No. Get me out! I'll do anything, Crawford, admit anything. You were right. I'm no doctor. I had two years in France and they dismissed me. The opium. There. Now. I've told you—" His babble broke off in a wild shriek. Crawford had not seen the snake strike. It fell away from Huerta's back, slithering off into the thicket. Huerta crawled toward Crawford on his hands and knees, a faint, yellow froth forming at his lips. He clutched at Crawford's legs, shouting up at him. "I'll tell you anything, please, anything. I was the one who killed Otis Rockland. Is that what you want? I knew Tarant had given him that piece of the *derrotero,* and I knew Otis was in that hotel room. I'd just reached him when you arrived, and I had to escape by the balcony without getting the map—"

Again his hoarse bawling broke off in a scream. His struggles had carried them both over to a thicket, and Crawford could see the same snake Huerta did, coiled almost at their feet. He tore free of the doctor's frantic hands, throwing himself back, and firing at the serpent. He tripped and fell heavily onto his back, seeing the snake jerk with the slug but reach Huerta anyway. Screaming, the doctor fought to gain his feet.

"Get me out, Crawford, get me out," he howled, pawing the writhing, thumping thing off in horror, whirling to run blindly away from it across the small opening. "It wasn't Quartel who had Whitehead try

to bushwhack you that time, either. It was me. I wanted
the third of the *derrotero* you had. And I was the one
who tried to get Merida's third in the house during the
bull-tailing. Please, Crawford, what more can you
want? Get me out now!"

He looked like some frenzied beast, greasy black
hair down over his face, froth drooling off his chin. He
stumbled blindly into a *mogote* of chaparro *prieto,* and
tried to turn and get out. But there must have been a
nest of them in the black chaparral, and they caught him
there.

"No, Crawford," he screamed, as the first one struck,
with a fleshy spississitude, knocking him to his knees in
the thicket, "they're all around me," and his voice broke
as a second one caught him. "For Christ's sake, Crawford,
get me out. I told you, didn't I?" he sobbed, trying to
crawl on through. And then another one struck him.
"Oh, for God's sake, Crawford, please, for God's sake."
And another, and he was lying on his belly, still trying
to crawl, and his voice had sunk to a pitiful wailing, like
a little child weakening, sinking until it was barely
audible. "Please, get me out, oh, please, Crawford, get me
out," and then dying finally, beneath the crescendo
hissing of the snakes, "Get me out, I'll do anything, only
please get me out—"

After it had ceased, Crawford felt himself twitch, and
realized how long he had been crouching there in a dazed
shocked immobility at such a bizarre, terrifying display.
It was like awakening from a deep sleep. There was a
thick, sweet taste in his mouth, and he was sweating, and
movement came with a strange pain. He saw that Merida
was standing over him, staring at the brush with that
same stunned horror in her face. His movement caused
her to turn in something akin to surprise. She looked at
him a moment before her eyes dropped to his hand; he
was rising, but the sound she made stopped him. It must

have struck him sometime during his struggles with Huerta. He did not remember when. The twin red punctures on the back of his hand were oozing blood thickly. With a curse, he started to rise again and get the rifle, but Merida caught him.

"No, Crawford. The knife. Your bowie. You've got to get it now before it spreads." She was on her knees beside him, pulling the bowie from his boot where he had thrust it after winding those strips of blanket on.

"The snakes," he said, "the snakes—"

"If we sit still they won't come for a minute. Now—I've got to." She met his eyes, then bent over his hand with the blade. He felt himself turn rigid, but it caused him less pain than he anticipated. She did it in three quick, skillful strokes. "I told you my mother was a *curandera*. I've seen her do this a dozen times. Find some Spanish dagger and you can get a poison from it that makes as good an antidote as any."

She bent to suck the wound, and now it was beginning to come. *Take it easy.* The hissing bore in on him with a physical weight. *Take it easy, damn you. That's why Huerta's through. He lost his head. All right. Get up, then, damn you, get up.* He got up.

The motion drew his hand from Merida's fingers, and she rose too. He had scooped up the Henry in rising, and he pulled the lever down. No fired shell popped out, and he realized the magazine must be empty. He reached in his right-hand pocket for fresh loads, and pulled out his hand, empty. The woman's eyes followed the movements in a fascinated way as he shifted the rifle so he could reach into his left-hand pocket. Again his hand came out empty. Merida's gaze raised to his, and they stared at each other blankly for a long moment. A small, hopeless sob escaped her.

The first, faint, snapping crackle came from behind, turning him that way. It was a big diamondback, slithering from the switch mesquite. It stopped as it caught sight of them, and its long, shimmering body coiled with oily facility. The ugly hammerhead raised, and the glittering opacity of its cruel little eyes held Crawford's gaze in a viscid mesmerization. Then it began to rattle.

"Crawford—"

The woman's agonized whisper brought his eyes around the other way. Another serpent, as big around as his lower leg, had crawled from a *mogote* of huisache. Again it was the soft snap of decaying vegetation that lay thickly over the ground, and the cessation of this as the snake saw them and stopped, and that swift coiling movement, and that sibilant rattle.

"Crawford," said Merida, in a hoarse, strained whisper. "We can't move. They'll strike as soon as we move. They're all around us and we can't move—"

"No," he said gutturally. "Remember they don't often strike above the hip. You've got those batwings. Just keep your feet, that's all, just keep your feet."

"There's another one," she said, and he saw the panic was gripping her the way it had Huerta. "We can't move, Crawford. Not a step. They'll have us."

"Merida," he said. "You've got to. Don't lose your head. Just start walking."

"I can't," she said, in a strangled, pathetic way, "Crawford, I can't—"

He could feel that animal fear rising up in him, to blot out all his terrible control. Sweat formed gleaming streaks through the grime of his face. His right hand was clenched so hard around the useless gun it ached. Gritting his teeth, he summoned the awful, supreme effort of will it would take for him to make that first step. His whole body was stiffened for it, when the first thunderous detonation came from out in the brush. There was a second, and a third, before Crawford recognized them as gunshots. This was followed by a long crashing of brush,

and Quartel burst into view. This movement caused the
snake on Crawford's right to strike. It hit his leg with a
solid thump, knocking him over against Merida, and
though he knew the fangs had not penetrated the triple
thickness of Chimayo blanket around his calf, he could
not hold back his hoarse, fearful shout. Quartel had
fired twice at the second rattler, knocking it back before
it could strike. The serpent tried to recoil and strike
again, in a weak, abortive way, and Quartel jumped at it
with a curse, stamping on its head. Then he whirled
away to fire at a third one beyond Merida.

"Hola!" bellowed Quartel. "Let's go. You only got
a little stretch left and we'll be out."

"You!" said Crawford blankly, gaping at him.

"Who else?" grinned the man. He caught Crawford
by the shoulder, shoving him forward. "Come on, I tell
you. We ain't got time for coffee."

The rest of it was Quartel's bellowing gun and the
crash of mesquite and Merida's hoarse, uncontrollable
sobbing and a nightmarish sense of movement within and
without him as he staggered through the thickets. At
last he found himself face down on gritty sand, his breathing settling down to the shallow exhalation of complete
exhaustion. He looked up to see Quartel squatting over
him, that grin on his sweaty, greasy face. The woman
was sitting up on the bank beyond Quartel, the batwings
lying at her feet. Crawford realized he was barefooted
and the blanketing had been stripped off his legs.

"The chaps saved Merida," said Quartel. "And that
Chimayo on you was a good idea. The only thing you
got is that hand. I don't think it will cause you too much
trouble, the way she fixed it."

"Why did you come back?" said Crawford.

Quartel shrugged. "For the same reason you gave me
those shells back in the bog when you didn't know for
sure whether I'd use them on you or the snakes, I guess."

He sat there looking at Crawford a while. "I'm sort of glad it was Huerta that killed Rockland," he said finally. He laughed, at the look Crawford gave him. "*Sí*. You could have heard that Huerta yelling up in San Antone. My horse went down just as I got out, and I was lying here in the sand when Huerta cut loose. He really cracked up good, didn't he? It sort of finishes my job out here."

Merida came over and lowered herself to her knees beside Crawford, and he sat up, staring at Quartel. "Your job?"

That pawky grin was on the Mexican's face. "*Sí*. Like I said I knew one who pinned it to his undershirt. Me, I couldn't even do that. Only a damn fool would come into the *brasada* with a badge. But I got a commission back in San Antonio from the federal government."

Crawford continued to stare at the man a long time, and it all went through his head, before he said it. "*Marshal* Quartel?"

"That's right," said the Mexican. "Maybe I look like I should be a *rurale*, but I'm a citizen of the States and my father was before me. They sent me out to get you a couple of weeks after Rockland was killed. Other lawmen had been given the job without meeting much success. I guess you know about that. I figured you'd turn up at your old corral sooner or later, so I had the Nueces Cattle Association recommend me to Tarant as qualified to rod the roundup he was managing for Rockland's estate. By the time you'd showed up at the Big O, I'd been there long enough to find out that, whether you murdered Rockland or not, there was more to the whole business than just the personal trouble between you and him. That *derrotero* for instance. I'd gotten a third of it from Whitehead. He'd found it many years ago on the body of one of the Mexican muleteers, who had been shot in the brush by Houston's men but apparently had gotten away from them to die. It was the section of the map which showed Snake Thickets, and how to find the chests once you got inside the thickets, but not how to find the thickets themselves. When you finally arrived, I had to choose between nabbing you then, or staying on and trying to find out what was really behind the murder."

"Then, those other lawmen—"

"The ones I told you about when I found you at Delcazar's?" Quartel giggled slyly. "I'm the only lawman I seen in the *brasada* since I came. You were pretty jumpy, Crawford. I thought if I cinched the girth up tight enough it might squeeze out some interesting things."

There was no apology in his voice for how he had used Crawford. The elemental brutality of the man was in his greasy, thick-featured face, and the courage, too. *And it would take that kind,* thought Crawford, *to come into a place like this. I can cuss better and ride better and rope better than any hombre in the world.*

"Not rope better."

"What?" said Quartel.

"Nothing," said Crawford, sitting up to pull on his boots. "How about Tarant?"

"He was involved all right," said Quartel. "He knew Rockland had that section of the map, and allowed Huerta to stay at the Big O, undoubtedly having made some deal with him to split the money when they got it. Since it was Huerta that murdered Rockland, we might be able to nab Tarant as an accessory."

With a weary breath, Crawford rose. "We can reach Del's from here in a couple of hours. He needs tending to, and that old Chihuahua cart of his will be better than walking back."

Quartel got up and turned to climb the bank toward the brush. Merida started after him, but Crawford caught her arm.

"Out there in the thickets," he said. "I didn't quite get it. You were all mixed up. Something about not knowing what you'd wanted all your life, and knowing now."

"Maybe seeing those chests of gunpowder made me realize it fully," she said. "It could be symbolical, in a way, of money. You seek it all your life, and when you finally get it, you realize it isn't what you want, after all."

"What *do* you want?"

"Don't you know?"

He gazed at her without speaking for a moment. Her face had taken on that feminine softness. Her eyes met his widely, shining a little. He was suddenly swept with the desire to shout or cry or laugh or take her in his arms, he didn't know which, the realization swelled so swiftly within him. It had all been so broken and aborted and bitterly frustrating between himself and Merida before, and now it was so complete. Yet, somehow, it was too poignant to express here. He reached out and took her hand.

"Let's go," he said.

Les Savage, Jr. was an extremely gifted writer who was born in Alhambra, California, but grew up in Los Angeles. His first published story was *Bullets and Bullwhips* accepted by the prestigious Street and Smith's *Western Story Magazine*. Almost ninety more magazine stories all set on the American frontier followed, many of them published in Fiction House magazines such as *Frontier Stories* and *Lariat Story Magazine* where Savage became a superstar with his name on many covers. His first novel, *Treasure of the Brasada*, appeared in 1947, the first of twenty-four published novels to appear in the next decade. Due to his preference for historical accuracy, Savage often ran into problems with book editors in the 1950s who were concerned about marriages between his protagonists and women of different races — a commonplace on the real frontier but not in much Western fiction in that decade. As a result of the censorship imposed on many of his works, only now have they been fully restored by returning to the author's original manuscripts. *Table Rock*, Savage's last book, was even suppressed by his agent in part because of its depiction of Chinese on the frontier. It has now been published as he wrote it by Walker and Company in the United States and Robert Hale, Ltd., in the United Kingdom.

Savage died young, at thirty-five, from complications arising out of hereditary diabetes and elevated cholesterol. However, his considerable legacy lives after him, there to reach a new generation of readers. His reputation as one of the finest authors of Western and frontier fiction continues and is winning new legions of admirers, both in the United States and abroad. Such noteworthy titles as *Silver Street Woman, Outlaw Thickets, Return to Warbow, The Trail* and *Beyond Wind River* have become classics of Western fiction. His most recent books are *Copper Bluffs* (1995), *The Legend of Señorita Scorpion* (1997), *Fire Dance at Spider Rock* (1995), *Medicine Wheel* (1996), *Coffin Gap* (1997), *Phantoms in the Night* (1998) and *The Bloody Quarter* (1999).